TIME OFF FOR ROMANCE

All the way from Bryson General Hospital to the luxurious Desert Plaza Hotel, Paulette Castle dreamed of the ten-day vacation ahead—a magic oasis time of sun and fresh air, away from her past and Jim Owens.

However, relief from nursing and romance was the last thing she was to find at the Desert Plaza. Instead, there was an attractive young doctor who desperately needed an office nurse, and something more . . . something that made Paulette afraid, for he had an inner turmoil of his own which she could not even begin to understand.

How could she comprehend the riddle of this man, when her own heart was still such a mystery?

NURSE ON LEAVE

ARLENE HALE

ACE BOOKS, INC.
1120 Avenue of the Americas
New York, N.Y. 10036

I

THE CLOCK read three forty-five and Paulette Castle, R.N., hadn't got away from the hosptal yet. One of the nurses on the three o'clock shift was late and Paulette crossed her fingers. If something came up and she had to work extra time—she sighed. Maybe the vacation was too good to be true. She knew that right this minute Irma Wyse, her roommate, was probably pacing the floor and chewing her nails. Irma was the nervous type.

"Something will happen at the last minute, I just know it!" Irma had been wailing for a week. "You just wait and see."

"Honestly, Irma, must you be such a crepe hanger?" Paulette had replied with a laugh. "The vacation is planned and it will come off as scheduled."

"The Desert Plaza!" Irma sighed, ruffling her short cropped dark hair. "I just can't believe it. I won't believe it until we're actually there and lounging around that wonderful hotel room."

The vacation was going to cost them a small mint, but they had been saving scrupulously for what seemed like years now to be able to go. Paulette had heard of the place through a wealthy patient and the more she had heard, the more she wanted to go.

The desert with its stretches of open, quiet country, the majestic saguaro cacti reaching its prickly arms to the clean sky, the mountains nearby with rugged peaks hiding secrets of lost gold mines and the magnificent sunsets—all of this would seem like heaven after the hectic, short-handed, exhaustive hours on the floor of Bryson General Hospital.

"Where *is* Johnson?" Paulette asked impatiently.

"Steady, girl," the Super said. "She'll be along."

"The question is, when?" Paulette grinned. "If I don't get home soon, poor Irma—"

The Super didn't know Irma, but she had heard enough about her to laugh and make a face.

"When does your train leave?"

"Nine forty."

"You've oodles of time."

Oodles of time! But if Johnson didn't show—well, she absolutely couldn't fill in for anyone. Doing double duty was hard enough any time, but today it was unthinkable.

"Relax, Paulette; here comes Johnson," the Super said.

Johnson was coming down the hall ninety per and was puffing for breath.

"Good grief, Paulette, I'm sorry! Of all days, I had a flat. I couldn't get a cab and I had to come on the city bus and you know how slow they are!"

"It's okay." Paulette breathed a sigh of relief. "You're here and that's all that matters."

"Have a good vacation."

"I intend to!" Paulette laughed.

"Catch a handsome man while you're at it," Johnson called after her as she hurried down the hall, rubber soles whispering over the floor.

"A millionaire, no less!" Paulette replied with a grin.

The elevator swished her down to first and she stepped out into the lobby. But it wasn't until she had crossed the parking lot and got in her car that she actually felt a free woman. Two glorious weeks of freedom! Two weeks of seeing no one suffer, two weeks of thinking like a girl on vacation instead of a nurse.

The drive to the small apartment she shared with Irma Wyse, an old childhood friend, was a short one. Irma was watching for her.

"I've nearly died of heart failure," she gasped. "I thought you weren't ever going to come."

"Johnson was late, wouldn't you know," she explained. "But I'm here now and there's no reason to get yourself all worked up over nothing."

"Nothing! Nothing! If we miss that train tonight, everything goes haywire!"

"We'll make it."

Irma had a light lunch ready for them and they sat down to eat, so excited neither of them really tasted the sandwiches or black coffee that Irma made as strong as a witch's brew.

Despite the fact that they had a few hours, it went quickly, with showering, last minute packing, phone calls and taking a cab to the station.

The train was miraculously on time and before they knew it they were on their way, speeding across the country, heading for the desert.

"I don't believe it!" Irma sighed. "I'm dreaming!"

"You're not dreaming and we *are* on our way," Paulette answered.

Irma groped around in her purse and came up with a much read and nearly tattered brochure that described the Desert Plaza.

"Imagine, breakfast served in our room. Moonlight horseback rides. Swimming. Golf. Tennis. Men!"

Paulette laughed and peered at the brochure. "I doubt they guarantee that last item, Irma."

"I can hope, can't I?"

"Of course. I wish you luck."

Irma frowned, her small face studious. "What about you, Paulette?"

"I only want rest and some quiet. A little fun. You know that."

Irma snapped her purse shut. "It's still Jim with you, isn't it? When are you going to snap out of it, kiddo?"

Paulette turned away to stare out the train window, watching the fields go by. Jim! Jim Owens. It was best not to think about him. It was over. So completely over that she would carry the scars of it for the rest of her life.

He was one of the reasons she wanted to take this vacation. In Bryson she was constantly reminded of him, of places they used to visit, things they used to do. Occasionally she ran into some of Jim's friends and it was awkward. None of them knew what to say and neither did she. Jim was seeing someone else now. It was rumored it was getting serious.

At least at the Desert Plaza she could look at unfamiliar places and see no one but strangers. She hoped fervently that in these next two weeks she could come to grips with herself. She needed to do that more than anyone knew. Not even Irma realized how deeply she had been cut.

Irma chatted as the train click-clacked along. Later they went to the club car and munched on a sandwich. Then they settled down in their coach seats for some sleep. If their budget had allowed, they would have taken a sleeper, but they had to trim corners somewhere.

Paulette was tired with the busy day behind her and as a nurse on call she had learned to sleep and relax whenever she could. Irma didn't relax well. She complained that her back ached and she wiggled constantly. Both were glad when they saw the dawn break. The countryside had changed. In another few hours they would be deep in the heart of the desert.

When they went to eat breakfast, the diner held an assortment of interesting people and Irma scanned them all for prospects.

"Now there's one for you!" she said, nudging Paulette. "And he's looking at us."

"Irma, shh!" Paulette said. "He'll hear you."

"Isn't he handsome!" Irma sighed.

Despite herself, Paulette had to smile. Irma was so uninhibited. She was apt to say or do anything. Perhaps that was why Paulette had always liked her. Irma was the life of the party and things never grew dull around her.

The man she had spied was just leaving his table. He was tall, blond, and nice looking. His eyes were gray and his clothes were well cut, expensive. He had the look of an eastern executive about him. Dropping some change to the table, he prepared to go.

As he passed their table, he nodded and smiled. "Good morning, girls."

"Good morning," Irma replied brightly. "Isn't it a lovely day?"

He murmured something and walked on. Paulette followed him with her eyes until the door swung shut behind him. She would probably never see him again but she was certain she would never forget him. There was a certain distinction about him, or was it his smile? It was the same with some of her patients. Some made deep impressions; others for one reason or another did not.

When the last of their coffee was finally gone, they returned to their seats. Irma scanned their fellow travelers for the interesting man, but he wasn't among them.

"He'll be traveling in a compartment, honey," Paulette told her.

"I suppose so. And he's probably got a wife and five kids. Just my luck."

Paulette gave her friend a wink. "But just wait until you get to the Desert Plaza."

"Hmm," Irma said, settling back with a smile.

The time went quickly and they began to gather their things for the next stop, Sweet Springs, the one they had been waiting for.

9

Half an hour later, they were standing on the platform of the desert town.

"Over there. There's the Desert Plaza station wagon," Irma said.

The uniformed driver took their luggage and stowed it away.

"Are we the only passengers?" Irma asked.

"I have one more, Miss. He'll be along in a minute."

They sat in the station wagon waiting, impatient to be on their way. The Desert Plaza was a few quick miles out of Sweet Springs.

"Sorry to keep you waiting," a strong male voice said.

Irma gaped and even Paulette felt a whisper of surprise. It was the man they had seen on the train.

"Good morning, girls."

"Hello," Irma replied.

"Good morning," Paulette nodded.

"Beautiful day," he said.

They murmured their agreement. As the station wagon pulled away the man twirled his hat in his hands.

"I guess we're all bound for the same place. My name is Sheridan, Boyd Sheridan."

Irma took care of the introductions and Paulette noticed that Boyd's gray eyes lingered for a moment on her face.

"Vacationing long at the Plaza?" he asked.

"Ten days," Paulette replied.

"Good. I'll be there a couple of weeks. Maybe we'll see each other again. Been there before?"

"No," Irma answered. "But we've been told it's a fabulous place."

"I see," Boyd replied with a nod of his head.

Then he turned his attention to the countryside that was slipping by outside the window and said no more. It was a short ride to the Plaza from Sweet Springs. As the driver approached, slowing down, they caught a glimpse of the very modern hotel building, the clear, sparkling water in the pool, and the white-clad figures on the tennis courts.

The brochure hadn't done it justice. It was even more

lovely—beautifully landscaped, and with the desert background, the mountains rising nearby, it was like something out of a fantasy.

"Impressive," Boyd Sheridan murmured. "Very impressive."

When the station wagon pulled up under the canopy, a uniformed doorman opened their door. Bellhops came to look after their luggage and in a matter of minutes the girls had been officially welcomed and taken to their rooms.

"Oh!" Irma gasped, wide-eyed. "This is wonderful!"

Paulette tipped the boy and closed the door. The carpet was thick and luxurious. The twin beds were oversize. Sliding glass doors and rich draperies took up one entire side of the room. Opening them, they stepped out to their own private balcony and found themselves overlooking the green lawns and a patio where tables were set. Just beyond that was the pool.

Further investigation proved the Desert Plaza had overlooked nothing for their comfort.

"Good heavens," Irma cried out. "Look at this bathroom, Paulette. It's bigger than our entire bedroom at home."

"Right now, I could soak for an hour in that tub," Paulette replied. "It's nice, Irma. Real nice. I love it here already."

"Me too. But I'm hungry. Isn't it lunch time?"

Paulette checked her watch. "Yes, it is. Let's change and go find the dining room."

Everything in the hotel more than lived up to their expectations. They ate cold salads and sandwiches on the lawn at one of the patio tables. Piped in music drifted out to them, along with muffled shouts from the pool.

Suddenly Irma kicked Paulette under the table.

"Get a load of that one," she whispered. "He's giving me the eye and I wish he'd stop it!"

Paulette tossed a casual glance over her shoulder and saw what Irma meant. He was clearly ogling them and when he caught Paulette's glance, he was on his feet and coming toward them.

"Oh, good grief!" Irma wailed.

"He's all yours, honey," Paulette laughed. "You came to the Desert Plaza for excitement and here it comes."

"Hello, girls. Staying here at the Plaza? So am I. Let me introduce myself. My name's Hinkle. George Hinkle. Everyone calls me George."

Without being asked, George pulled up a chair, sat down at their table and asked their names. Irma supplied them.

"What's your poison, girls? Riding, swimming, golf?"

"Everything," Irma said airily.

"Well," George said, rubbing his hands briskly. "I'm just your man. Be glad to show you girls around. There's a dance tonight. How about it? Be glad to escort you."

Paulette glanced at Irma. But Irma, despite all her talk, was careful of the men she dated.

"Sorry, George, but we just got in and we're tired. We won't make any promises about the dance."

George was not especially good-looking, but he smiled often. Off to one side of his mouth, Paulette caught a flash of gold in his teeth. His black hair was thinning on top and he looked as if he needed some body-building exercises. He looked soft, as if he made it a habit of frequenting places like the Desert Plaza.

"Now, girls, let's be friends," George said with a nervous little laugh.

"We'll keep your offer in mind," Irma replied.

George looked from one to the other and lifted his shoulders in a slight shrug.

"Well, nice meeting you girls. See you around."

Then he said goodbye and ambled away. Irma made a face at Paulette.

"There's always one of those around," she giggled. "Poor George! I bet he's asked every woman in the hotel for a date tonight."

"I wish him luck," Paulette replied.

After lunch, they strolled the grounds together, pausing for awhile to watch a tennis game. At the pool, everyone lay lazily in the sun, tanning their skins to a coppery color.

Suddenly they heard from the loudspeaker, "Doctor Lane.

12

Please come to your office. Doctor Lane. Paging Doctor Lane."

Paulette saw one of the sunbathers leap to his feet. He was a thin, tall man. Snatching up his towel, he hurried away.

"House doctor?" Irma wondered. "Or guest?"

"Maybe there's an emergency of some kind," Paulette said with a frown, watching the doctor until he was out of sight.

"Nothing doing, kiddo. You're on vacation, remember. Besides, if they have a doctor here, they've already got a nurse. You couldn't possibly be needed."

Paulette laughed. "You're right, Irma. I hung up my uniform for two whole weeks. Hey, how about a swim?"

"Sounds wonderful."

They went back to the hotel and when they got on the elevator, they saw the doctor again.

"I've got to get dressed," he told the elevator operator. "I thought I was going to have a quiet afternoon."

"No such thing, Doctor Lane."

All of them got off on the third floor. The doctor hurried away and disappeared into a room at the end of the hall. As Paulette unlocked her door, she heard the phone ringing. Dashing to answer it, she heard a strong male voice again and knew instantly that it was Boyd Sheridan.

"Miss Castle? There's a dance tonight. I'd like very much to take you, How about it?"

II

BOYD SHERIDAN was a handsome man and probably an interesting one. The dance would no doubt be fun too. But Paulette knew what her answer would be.

"I'm sorry, Mr. Sheridan. I thank you for the offer, but I don't believe so tonight."

It was apparent that Mr. Sheridan was surprised. It took a moment for him to regain himself. "You're positive, Miss Castle?"

"Yes. Thank you again."

"Oh. Well then, goodbye."

The receiver clicked in Paulette's ear. Irma stood staring at her, feet planted far apart, hands on her hips, mouth agape.

"You turned down Boyd Sheridan!"

Paulette turned away and went out to stand on the balcony. She didn't want to argue about it. The simple truth was, she couldn't endure a date with another man. Not just yet. There were too many painful memories of Jim still in her heart. Irma's step was light beside her.

"Sorry, Paulette. I guess you know what you're doing."

"Yes."

"Hey, we were going swimming, remember?" Irma asked cheerfully. "Let's get in our suits and go."

Half an hour later, well oiled against the sun's bright rays, sunglasses covering their eyes, they stretched side by side near the edge of the pool. Both of them dropped off to sleep for a few minutes, tired from their all-night ride on the train.

Both awakened at the sound of a noisy car pulling up to the hotel. Raising herself up on her elbows, Paulette took off her sunglasses and peered with a puzzled smile.

"What kind of car is that?" Irma asked.

"Beats me," Paulette replied.

The car was old and rattly. It jarred the atmosphere here. The broad-shouldered fellow who climbed out of it with aplomb acted as if it were a Cadillac. Wearing boots, faded denims and a dusty hat, he took his battered bag and tromped into the hotel.

"Takes all kinds," Irma murmured. "How can he afford to stay here?"

"How can we?" Paulette replied.

They laughed at that and forgot about the new arrival. For one thing, George Hinkle was bearing down on them again.

"Hello, hello, hello!" he waved gaily.

In a swimming suit he left much to be desired. Plunking down beside Irma, he began to talk to her, telling her amusing little anecdotes about customers who had come to the Desert Plaza over the last few years.

"I come every year," he said. "Love the place. Just crazy about it! Say, Irma, my love, are you sure you don't want to go to the dance with me?"

"You'd step on my new shoes," Irma retorted in her friendly way.

"Risk it! Live dangerously!"

Paulette turned her face away to hide a smile. George wasn't exactly date bait, but he would do in a pinch. That's exactly what Irma was thinking. Besides, he would get her into circulation. She wasn't surprised when Irma finally agreed.

George wandered away then, whistling, stopping to talk to everyone around the pool.

"What made me do that?" Irma asked, fuming at herself.

"Once won't hurt," Paulette answered.

"You sure you don't mind? Our first night—"

"We promised each other there would be none of that

sort of thing, remember? We came for fun. I know you love to dance. Go and have fun."

"What will you do?"

Paulette ran a hand over her red hair, knowing what the sun would do to it. It would be as burnished as a copper kettle.

"I don't know yet. But you're not to think about me for a second, pal. Understand?"

Irma wrinkled her pug nose at her and grinned. "You're a brick, Paulette."

The sun was relaxing. Irma, the restless type, was in and out of the water a dozen times to Paulette's two. Abruptly, it seemed the heat of the sun was gone. Opening her eyes, Paulette looked around her. Everyone else had left. The pool was quiet. The sun was dropping in the westward sky.

"Let's go too," Paulette said.

Irma was sunburned. Despite all the care they had taken, she was beet red.

"Fine care you took of me!" Irma chided with a grin.

"I brought some lotion with me. Just don't let George pat you on the back tonight."

"If that guy even looks like he's going to touch me—"

Paulette draped the towel around her shoulders, pushed her toes into thongs and thought with longing of a cool bath in the luxurious tub in their room.

In the dining room that evening, Paulette saw Boyd Sheridan. He was dining alone. He acknowledged them with a curt nod of his head. Seeing him dressed in a white dinner jacket and a correct bow tie, he cut a striking picture. On a dance floor he would probably be superb.

As they finished their dessert, George Hinkle joined them.

"Doll, you look real pretty," he told Irma. "Sunburn and all."

"Gee, thanks," Irma said with mock pleasure.

George grinned, the gold in his teeth flashing. "You're one of those cute ones, aren't you?"

Paulette pushed back from the table. "If you two will excuse me—"

16

She walked away with her long-legged stride. The dance would be starting soon in the ballroom. She would spend the evening in her room with one of the books she had brought along.

Locking the door behind her, she kicked off her shoes, opened the sliding doors so fresh desert air came in, and propped herself up on the roomy bed.

After one chapter, she was bored. Here she was in the fabulous Desert Plaza, reading a dull book!

With disgust, she threw it across the room. It was true she was tired and it was true she didn't want to date anyone, but this was still not her idea of a vacation. She could have fun without getting involved, couldn't she?

Leaving her room once again, she decided to take a walk. The air here was delightful. There were horses somewhere on the place. Maybe she could find the stable and look at them.

As she strode toward the elevator, a door flew open.

"You! In here! Quick!"

Paulette halted her steps. "I beg your pardon—"

"In here!"

A hand came out and grabbed her by the wrist. She started to scream but checked herself when she saw it was the doctor.

"I need help," he said. "This woman is having a stroke. Here, take this wooden depressor and hold her tongue down. I've got to give her a shot. Move, Miss. Move!"

Everything came into sharp focus for Paulette then. She had seen things like this before. Taking the wooden depressor from the doctor's hand, she placed it in the woman's mouth and pressed down, holding the tongue in place. With a stroke there was always a danger that the patient would swallow his tongue and choke to death.

The doctor's face was anxious as he readied the syringe.

"How's she doing?" he asked.

"Fine, doctor."

"Thank God you happened along. You handle that depressor like a veteran."

17

Paulette smiled faintly. "I am. I'm a registered nurse."

The doctor's eyes were surprised for a moment and then he administered the shot.

"My luck must be changing," he said. "My office nurse is away for a few days and I knew it would mean all sorts of emergencies. But with you here—"

"I'm on vacation, Doctor," Paulette pointed out.

"I'll need you for awhile yet, at least until I can get an ambulance here from Sweet Springs. Get on the phone, will you? The number is there in the book. Can't remember it. Haskins Ambulance Service."

Paulette would have resented the doctor's crisp orders at any other time, but she knew the patient should be taken to the hospital as quickly as possible.

It took only a few seconds to get the ambulance service and they promised to come immediately. Paulette hung up. Doctor Lane was still checking his patient, watching closely.

"I take it you're the house doctor here, Doctor Lane."

"I am," he said crisply. "Who are you?"

"Miss Castle. Paulette Castle."

"This lady has no one here with her. Would you ride in the ambulance with her to the hospital? I'll follow in my car. As soon as I have her settled, I'll drive you back."

"Of course," Paulette replied.

They looked at each other for a moment and the doctor's thin face lighted with a smile.

"Sorry if I ruined your first night here, Miss Castle."

"How did you know it was my first night?"

"I saw you arrive," he replied. "Why don't you see if you can't pack a few things for Mrs. Adams? I'm sure she'll want them."

"All right."

Paulette gathered together a few personal items and put them in a small bag she found in the closet. By the time she had finished and the two of them had searched her handbag for the name of someone in her immediate family, the ambulance came screeching up to the side entrance.

Paulette helped put Mrs. Adams on the stretcher and followed, carrying the small bag. The arrival of the ambulance had attracted a crowd and Paulette saw Irma.

"What's going on?" Irma asked. "Where are you going?"

"I'll be back shortly. The doctor needs me," Paulette explained.

Irma shook her head. "We haven't been here six hours and already you're the same as back in uniform!"

Paulette gave her friend a smile and climbed into the ambulance. Mrs. Adams was settled comfortably and Paulette sat beside her, holding her hand. The old woman's eyes had fluttered open and Paulette smiled at her.

"You're going to be fine, Mrs. Adams. Doctor Lane and I will take care of you."

The old woman closed her eyes again.

The ambulance ran full speed, sirens blaring. They reached Sweet Springs in a very short time and rushed up to the emergency entrance of a small hospital. Paulette stood by while the attendants wheeled Mrs. Adams inside. In a matter of minutes, Doctor Lane was there too, giving directions, seeing her personally into a private room.

"I talked to the hotel manager before I left," Doctor Lane explained. "He knows Mrs. Adams quite well and gave me the name and address of her son. Would you put the call in for me, nurse?"

Paulette took the slip of paper he handed her and picked up the desk phone. The operator put the long distance call through and she heard the phone ringing several times. There was no answer.

It was two hours before Doctor Lane felt he could leave his patient. A special nurse had been called in. Mrs. Adams' son still could not be reached.

Doctor Lane took Paulette's arm and led her out of the hospital, down the steps and out to his car. It was a convertible—not new, not old, but very clean and polished.

"Thank you for giving up your evening, Miss Castle."

"I must say, I've never been grabbed out of a hall quite like that before," she said with a laugh.

Doctor Lane started the motor. "I'm sorry I had to be so brusque. Of all times for my office nurse to be away!"

The doctor turned his attention to the traffic and in a few short minutes they had left the town of Sweet Springs behind.

The desert road at night was cool and the stars seemed brighter than they did at home. With a large cactus looming up on the horizon here and there, it seemed a completely different world to Paulette and she sighed, just looking at it.

"First time to the desert?" he asked.

"Yes. I love it."

"Gets mighty warm sometimes," Doctor Lane said. "But I like it too. Hot and dry. Good for the lungs."

"Have you been house doctor at the Desert Plaza very long?"

"Six months," he replied crisply. "And if you're going to ask why I'm holding that job instead of some semi-retired man of seventy, don't bother. That happens to be my own business."

Paulette was startled by the sudden and abrupt anger in his voice. She had been wondering, of course. Good young doctors were needed everywhere, and it was true an older doctor could handle a place like the Desert Plaza.

"All right," she said coolly. "I won't ask."

"Good."

They drove on in silence. Now and then she stole a glance at him. He had a chin as hard as a rock and just as stubborn. Firm lips. A high forehead. A gaunt, hungry look around his eyes. He was much too thin. And his disposition wasn't the best in the world either.

They rolled into the Desert Plaza and for Paulette it was with a sense of relief.

As soon as he parked the car, Paulette climbed out of the car and began to walk away.

"Goodnight, Doctor."

"Hold on!" he called after her. "You don't have to go away in a huff."

Paulette stood her ground. This man blew hot one minute, cold the next. She was thoroughly confused.

"Come along. Let me buy you a cup of coffee at least. I guess I need one too. I didn't mean to bark at you back there. Honest."

He smiled at her. The hard chin softened and the eyes gleamed. She found herself smiling.

"All right, Doctor."

The dance was still going on. She wondered how Irma was making out with George, or if by now she had slapped his face and gone to her room.

To her surprise, the doctor led her straight toward the ballroom.

"But, Doctor—"

"Dancing is good exercise. Be good for both of us," he replied.

Just as they reached the door, they met Boyd Sheridan. He took them in with one quick, analyzing look. Then with a stiff nod of his head and a sardonical smile, he waved toward the music.

"Well, I yield to a better man," he said.

Paulette's cheeks burned with embarrassment. Doctor Lane was scowling, wondering what it was all about. Boyd Sheridan walked away, stiff and angry. She didn't know why a stranger's anger should bother her, but it did. It bothered her very much.

III

BOYD SHERIDAN tramped through the lobby angrily. Why seeing Paulette Castle with the house doctor should upset him so, he didn't know, but it did. If she'd already had a date

21

when he'd called her, why didn't she just say so? Somehow the tone in her voice had indicated to him that she simply wasn't interested in dating.

In the lobby, Boyd stopped at the cigar counter and bought a package of hard mints. Ever since he'd stopped smoking, he munched them, and especially when he was angry about something. Crushing them between his teeth had the same settling effect on him as a good smoke.

Jabbing the elevator button, he paced impatiently. What kind of service did they have in this hotel anyway?

At last the doors swished open. He glared at the elevator boy.

"Where were you, out to coffee?" he asked tartly.

The boy's ears turned red. Boyd stepped inside and folded his arms. Why had he snapped at the kid like that? There was no call for it. It was his own impatience that had made him angry.

When they reached the fifth floor, he reached in his pocket and found a coin. With an awkward gesture he dropped it in the boy's pocket.

"Sorry, fella. Just edgy tonight."

The boy grinned and Boyd felt somewhat better. "It's okay, sir. Maybe I was a little slow."

They smiled at each other and Boyd said goodnight. Taking his key, he opened the door to his suite. Although it was luxurious, it didn't really impress him. He had been in expensive suites before. By now he knew what things to look for in hotel rooms. It didn't take him long to classify them as excellent, standard or substandard.

The Desert Plaza would have to be classified as excellent. The Old Man would be happy to have that on his report. The Old Man! Boyd sighed deeply. Why did he take it? Why did he keep jumping when he barked at him? What was the matter with simply opening the door and walking out?

Boyd ripped open the draperies and stared out at the desert sky. At least the air was clean here, free of gasoline fumes and the smell of hot cement. He popped another mint in his mouth and loosened his tie. Shucking off his coat, he dropped it carelessly in a chair. If the Old Man saw him do that he'd yell his head off.

"Clothes cost money, boy. Don't you know that? Take care of things if you want to have a few thin dimes in this world!"

A few thin dimes. It was all the Old Man thought about. A few thin dimes! Boyd stepped out to his balcony and looked down below him. Music from the ballroom drifted up, sweet as the air, and he felt a kind of lonely restlessness stirring inside. He'd been feeling more and more like this lately. It was a new feeling. When had it all started? He didn't really know. At first everything was a bed of roses. College had been a lark. He'd never seriously studied, just skimming through. What was the need? The Old Man was loaded. A good job waited for him. He had it made. All he had to do was jump when the whip was cracked, say the right things at the right time and be prepared to lick the Old Man's boots. If he didn't, someone else would. That had been made plain to him.

A woman's laugh drifted up to him and he caught sight of a white dress, the man's white coat. Well, that wouldn't be Paulette Castle and the doctor. They hadn't been wearing formal attire. They had looked tired as a matter of fact, as if the doctor had been out on a case. Who was Paulette Castle? Besides an attractive red-headed girl with eyes that were cool but with hidden fires in them?

The phone rang and he jumped. Glancing at his watch, he knew it was probably the Old Man. He did half his business late at night and it would be nearly midnight in New York.

"Hello. Boyd Sheridan speaking," he answered.

"Boyd! Why haven't you called? I want that report and I want it fast!"

"I've been here less than twelve hours! What do you expect of me?"

There was a low laugh and he could see the Old Man shifting the big black cigar from one side of his mouth to the other. More than likely he was home, in the library, sitting at his huge desk, file folders open all over the place, with pads of paper full of scribbled notes.

The library had always been his father's sanctuary. As a boy, Boyd had been afraid to go in there. It was always full of strange men talking about things he didn't understand. When his father was making a business deal, the rest of the family were to stay out of his way. It had been a lesson hard learned, for by nature he had been a curious child, anxious to explore new horizons.

"Well, what's your first impression. Is it a good investment or not?"

"I don't like to make snap decisions—you know that," Boyd replied.

"You're hedging, boy!"

Boyd took a deep breath and felt the sweat on his brow, despite the air-conditioning in the room.

"I'm not hedging. I need more time."

There was a long pause. By picking up another phone, his dad could have someone else on his way out here in a matter of minutes. If that happened . . . Boyd sighed. He'd been called on the carpet before. It was unlike anything he had imagined. He had never known the Old Man could be so tough, so scathing, so demanding.

"I'll report tomorrow night, sir. A full report. But not until then. Take it or leave it!"

Boyd was surprised at himself. He had never spoken up to the Old Man that firmly before. There was another silence. He didn't know if he had stunned his father or if he were just gathering his forces together for another storm.

"Have your call in by ten tomorrow night. No later. I can't hold this deal up any longer. You got it?"

"Yes, sir!"

The receiver banged in Boyd's ear. With a sigh, Boyd sat down in a chair and rubbed his face tiredly. There wasn't much time to make an appraisal of the value of this place. And if his estimate happened to be wrong—well, he knew what that meant.

That was the worst of it. Half of him longed to please the

Old Man and wring one line of praise out of him, just once. The other half hated himself for knuckling under, letting his father treat him as he did.

Boyd began to undress. He had to get out of here and the best way to do that was on horseback. He had bought some Western clothes in a shop in the lobby earlier. Pulling them on now, feeling conspicuously like a dude, he stomped out to the hall and rang for the elevator. The same boy came up for him.

"Hey, neat, sir!" he said, ogling the new boots and the fancy, Western pants.

Boyd gave him a thin smile. The boy was trying to atone for what had happened before.

"You worked here long, son?" Boyd asked.

"Yes, sir, almost ever since it opened."

"Nice place. Business must be booming."

The boy nodded. "Pretty much, sir. I hear they're turning down reservations now."

Boyd's lips tightened. "I see."

"If you don't mind my saying so, sir, there's everything here anyone would want. Even a reducing salon!" he said with a grin.

Boyd smiled. "You're a good advertisement for the place."

The boy shrugged. "It's only the truth, sir."

"What's your name?"

"Johnny. Johnny Gates."

"I'll tell the manager to give you a raise," Boyd grinned.

They reached the lobby and Boyd walked across it quickly and outside. Swinging away to the right, he headed for a group of buildings where the horses were kept. They were some distance and he enjoyed the walk, stretching his long legs. But the more he walked, the madder he got. With everything. He hadn't wanted to make this trip to begin with. He was sick of appraising property for the Old Man. Sick of strange rooms and strange people. Sick of second-rate trains and too scared to ride airplanes. Sick of getting information on the sly.

"Let them know you're thinking of buying and the first

thing you know, the price goes up," the Old Man always said. "Take them by surprise and make a decent offer and most times, you can get it."

It wasn't unethical. Not really. It was just a smart way of operating. The Old Man knew all the smart ways and he had taught Boyd most of them. But that didn't mean he had to like it, Boyd thought angrily.

The stable was dark. No one was riding tonight, with the dance going on. He pounded on a door and finally heard someone stir inside. The man who peered out at him was probably in charge of the place. He looked a little disgruntled.

"What is it, mister?"

"I want a horse. The fastest, meanest one you've got."

"At this hour?"

Boyd stared him down. "At this hour. I believe your hotel advertises there are horses available for their guests!"

That did it. Just hint that the manager might hear of it and they jumped. Boyd grinned to himself. The man hustled away and threw a saddle on a black horse with white markings on his head and feet.

"We don't have any mean horses, mister. But this one is fast."

"No mean ones?" Boyd asked.

"We're careful to get gentle ones. Half the people that come here can't ride."

Boyd put his boot in the stirrup and swung up. This was something he had learned to do back in boy's camp and he had taken to it like a veteran. Even now, whenever he could, he slipped away to a saddle club and went riding. The Old Man thought it was an infantile sport. His idea of fun was to play poker with huge stacks of chips on either side of him. His most extensive exercise consisted of lifting his checkbook and having a rubdown in a steamroom.

Boyd took the reins in his hands, nudged the horse and they moved out.

"Better stick to the regular trails, mister!" the man yelled after him. "It's dark tonight."

Boyd ignored him. This was the best thing that had happened to him since he had left New York. He quickly spurred his horse into a gallop. The sound of hoofs bounding over the trail, the wind in his face, the strong horse beneath him—this all filled a need in him.

He galloped as fast as his horse could go until he was too tired to ride any further. Then he reined up sharply and dismounted. Both he and the horse were sweating and breathing hard. Boyd toook his hat off and lifted his face to the sky, feeling the breeze against his damp forehead and soaked shirt.

The stars were bright, the air clean. Just ahead he could make out the mountain peaks against the sky. Only a sliver of moon was shining.

A man should feel peace here, he thought. He had a horse, the open country, the sky, and not a soul in sight. Peace. Boyd's lips lifted in a wry smile. It *was* true a man's peace came from within.

He swung into the saddle and rode back to the stables much more slowly than he had come. Without waking the stablehand again, he put the horse in an empty stall, lifted off the saddle and rubbed him down. The horse nuzzled him and Boyd laughed softly.

"I like you too, fella. We'll go again."

The horse nickered and for a moment Boyd leaned his head against the strong shoulder of the animal. He felt the muscles quiver beneath his forehead and knotted his fingers in the silky mane. A horse was faithful at least. And he was honest. He either liked you or hated you and he let you know it.

"So long, fella," Boyd said.

He left the stable and walked back to the hotel. It was an odd oasis here in the middle of the desert. The bright lights were like beacons and the outlines of the modern building looked like some queer object that had sprouted up out of the ground.

The lobby was busy. The dance had ended. Boyd crowded into an elevator, aware of how he looked compared to the others. They were all returning to their rooms after the dance. Only one, a crew-cut, blue-jeaned and happy-looking young man, who wore impossibly shabby boots, appeared as if he hadn't been anywhere near the dance. In fact, Boyd wondered how he happened to be at the hotel at all. He looked more like a saddle bum.

"Been riding?" the man asked.

"Yes," Boyd replied.

"Should have done that, too, instead of tripping the light fantastic."

Boyd's eyebrows lifted. "You went to the dance?"

"Sure. Why not? There's one little gal there that really took my eye. But she was with George somebody or other. Her name's Irma Wyse. Know her?"

Paulette Castle's roommate!

"Yes, I know who she is," Boyd replied.

"My name's Allan. Mike Allan. What's yours, buddy?"

"Boyd Sheridan."

They shook hands. Boyd decided it took all kinds. How had Mike Allan scraped together enough money to come to the Desert Plaza?

The elevator stopped at three and some of the occupants got off. Boyd froze. There was Paulette Castle standing before Room Number 312. She wasn't alone. Doctor Lane was still with her. So they had stayed that long at the dance! The doctor was talking earnestly and Boyd scowled. Another minute and he would be kissing her, right there in front of everyone!

The door shut and Boyd breathed a sigh of relief. Mike Allan had been talking the whole while, but Boyd hadn't the slightest idea what he had said.

"Hey, wait!" Mike said suddenly. "This is my floor too. Off, please!"

The door came open again and Mike hurried off, calling goodnight. Boyd saw that Paulette and the doctor had disappeared. They must have gone inside her room. What for? A more private goodnight kiss?

Boyd ground his teeth together and groped in his pocket

for the mints. He popped three of them in his mouth and brought his teeth down hard.

Well, he could always tell the Old Man that the place had good romantic appeal. That was always a calling card for a resort area.

At the fifth floor, Boyd stalked out of the elevator and unlocked his door. It gave him little satisfaction to slam it shut with all his force. He heartily hoped he had managed to wake up someone, and if a quarrel resulted, he was ready for that too.

Pulling off his boots, he threw them into a closet and got out of his clothes. In the bathroom he turned on the shower and stepped under it. When the cold water had chilled him to the bone, he rubbed down and got into pajamas.

Then he picked up the phone and asked for Room 312. Paulette answered. She had a low, melodious voice. She said hello three times, sounding more puzzled each time. He couldn't say a thing. Feeling a fool, he simply hung up.

IV

IT WAS LATE. Paulette stretched luxuriously on the bed and watched Irma do all sorts of things to her face. When the last applications of lotion had been dabbed on with cotton, Irma put the cap back on the bottle and peered at herself in the mirror.

"I don't know why I keep trying," she sighed. "It's hopeless, Paulette. I'm always going to look like a friendly little puppy dog."

Paulette laughed at her friend's description of herself.

"What's cuter than a puppy dog?" she asked. "Besides, you had a date the very first night we were here. That's no reason to complain."

"George!" Irma wrinkled her nose. "George Hinkle. And he did step on my shoes. You'd think a gigolo like him would at least know how to dance!"

"What about the other one?" Paulette asked.

"Mike Allan? He's the one that drove up in that awful old car. And he took a real shine to me. But let's face it, Paulette. I can meet his sort at home. I only danced with him a couple of times anyway. George made it known I was *his* date!"

Paulette stretched again and wiggled her toes. She was tired. It had been a long day since they had left the train at Sweet Springs. Irma began doing some exercises, puffing with the effort.

"I'm just too lazy to join you," Paulette confessed. "Besides, if we go on that trail ride in the morning, that will be exercise enough for me."

Irma finished at last, doused the lights, and fell into bed with an exhausted sigh.

"So, okay, we know all about me and my evening. Now, I think it's time you did some explaining. I've been waiting for you to tell me."

"Tell you what?" Paulette asked with a grin.

Irma sputtered with anger. "You know what! How did you get involved with Doctor Lane? And for crying out loud, how did you get him to bring you to the dance?"

"Everything was his idea," Paulette replied. "He offered to buy me a cup of coffee, that's all. Then he took me straight into the dance."

"And?" Irma asked anxiously. "Well?"

"Well, nothing," Paulette shrugged. "We danced for quite awhile, and we did have the coffee and he saw me to our room. That's all."

"Look, kiddo, with a guy that looks like that, I wouldn't have let it end so easily."

Paulette laughed. "Oh, Irma, you talk big, but you're actually just a shy little kitten. Actually, he did step inside the room for a minute, but not for what you think. He dropped a coin and it rolled inside as we opened the door. He came in after it. That's all. As far as I'm concerned, Doctor Lane considered me a lucky replacement for a missing office nurse, nothing else."

"Oh, Paulette, you're not going to get all involved in patients and thermometers and shots and stuff, are you?"

"No," Paulette promised. "Not if I can help it. But you know, there's something funny about Doctor Lane."

"Funny?"

"What's he doing here, Irma? A good young doctor is needed in the hospitals or in private practice. Not in a plush resort like this."

"So maybe he likes this sort of set-up. Can't say I blame him."

"Such a waste," Paulette murmured. "Well, I'm for some shut-eye. You too, Irma. The trail ride starts early, you know."

The phone rang. Paulette jumped. It was so unexpected here. Groping for it, she answered. No one replied. She kept saying hello until the person on the other end hung up.

"Who was it?" Irma asked sleepily.

"Must have had the wrong room. Didn't answer. Goodnight, honey."

Sleep was sweet and deep, unclouded with dreams. It was the first night in ages that she hadn't dreamed about Jim Owens, and the whole trip was worth this much.

The alarm buzzed but Paulette was already awake. She shut it off and went to open the draperies and the sliding doors; although the room was air conditioned, she preferred the clean, natural air of the desert. She stepped out to the balcony and peered around her. The desert simmered in the early morning sun—flat, sandy and majestic. The mountains were rugged and harsh and blended with the natural beauty of the desert.

Irma was still sleeping soundly. Paulette called and Irma

didn't stir. Finally, Paulette shook her until her eyes opened and her pug nose twitched in protest.

"Get up, Irma. We've got a date with some horses, remember?"

"Do I have to get up?" Irma protested.

"You do unless you want to spend the morning here alone. Of course, George might keep you company—"

"That did it!" Irma exclaimed. "I'll get up."

A shower awakened them both and, pulling on their riding clothes, they giggled and laughed at each other. Paulette studied her lean, long figure in the mirror and grinned.

"Well, this is quite a change from a nurse's uniform."

"I'm starved," Irma announced.

They went down to the dining room. It wasn't hard to pick out those guests who were going on the trail ride with them, for they all wore appropriate garb. Boyd Sheridan was one of them. He barely glanced in their direction. Mike Allan wore the same sort of clothes he had worn yesterday. In fact, he had come to the dance dressed like this.

Of them all, Mike looked the most natural in boots, wide-brimmed hat and denims. He was another curiosity. Who was he and why was he here? Somehow he didn't quite blend with the rest of the clientele. But then, maybe she and Irma didn't either. It was certain that the Desert Plaza was too rich for their blood. They would go home flat broke. Most of the people who frequented the Desert Plaza were of the wealthy sort, out for a lark, or businessmen on vacation, rich girls bored with life and seeking new adventure, and the perennial resort set, like George Hinkle. Probably among the guests might be a few phonies, women seeking rich husbands or enterprising young men seeking rich wives. And us, Paulette thought with a smile, wanting fun, relaxation and in Irma's case, a few interesting dates. For herself, Paulette wanted only one thing. To forget Jim Owens, to steady herself, to get a new lease on life.

The breakfast was good. The desert air gave them an appetite. The morning was still cool and fresh, but by mid-morning the heat would begin to build up. This was one of the reasons the trail ride left so early. They would be back to the Plaza well before noon.

The social director of the hotel began to round up the riders and directed them to the stables some distance from the hotel.

"You think we should go?" Irma asked with a slight frown. "I haven't been on a horse since I was in fourth grade."

"Me either," Paulette laughed.

"You'll be all right, Miss," Mike Allan said, falling in step beside them. "I'll keep my eye on you. I know horses. I'll make certain they give you a gentle one."

"That's nice of you, Mr. Allan," Irma said.

"Mike. Call me Mike. Sure a pretty day, isn't it?"

"It's fabulous," Irma burst out enthusiastically. "It really is fabulous here."

Mike grinned and gave Irma a quick look of approval.

"I like the desert too. Fact is, I like the West. Period."

"You live in this part of the country?" Paulette asked.

Mike's eyes flickered. "Ma'am, I live wherever I hang my hat."

Paulette frowned. He had been deliberately evasive. She was certain of it. There was something a little out of step about Mike Allan, just as there was about Doctor Ross Lane.

The stables were full of horses, more horses than Paulette had ever seen at one time. They were saddled and ready for them. Mike quickly picked out two and helped Irma and Paulette mount up.

"If it's okay, I'll ride close by, Irma," he said.

"So you can pick up the pieces when I fall off?" Irma asked.

"Sure thing!" Mike laughed. "Only you won't fall. I'll catch you."

Mike was fussing with Irma's saddle, making certain it was securely fastened and shortening the stirrups a bit more.

"Are you a good rider?" a voice asked beside Paulette.

She turned in the saddle, knowing the voice. Boyd Sheridan had ridden over to her. His horse snorted and stamped impatiently. He sat the saddle well, like a trained horseman, and he was attractive in the Western garb, his eyes gray and quick under the brim of his hat.

"I'm afraid not," she answered.

"Better on the dance floor?" he wondered coldly.

Paulette straightened. He was still angry over last night. She took a deep breath. She didn't really want to explain, but she supposed that she must.

"I had no intention of going to the dance, Mr. Sheridan. I'm a nurse. Doctor Lane had an emergency and I helped him. The dance was his idea and if—"

She broke off. Why did she excuse herself to him? There was no need of it. It really was none of his business. But he smiled apologetically and she found herself smiling back.

"I'm sorry, Paulette. I've acted badly."

The trail ride was about to begin. Everyone was mounted and a weathered-looking man, who apparently had been around horses all his life, led them out. The trail was well beaten. How many riders had come this way—people like herself, looking for diversion?

Mike was riding beside Irma, talking in his quiet, easy voice. Now and then Irma laughed. The two of them seemed to hit it off very well.

Boyd stayed near Paulette and he talked of many things—recent books, movies, a little about art. This was a city man used to concerts, plays—the kind of entertainment a city had to offer. He was a man with money too. The boots he wore were expensive and the clothes were well cut.

"Mr. Sheridan, what business are you in?" Paulette asked.

He gave her a smile, a bare twitching of his lips. "I work for my father. He deals in any number of businesses. Anything that makes money interests him."

"I see," she murmured.

But she didn't really. It told her little. And why was he at the Desert Plaza? Was it for business reasons or was this strictly a vacation?

Irma was pointing and gesturing, seeing everything with quick, eager eyes. Some of her enthusiasm drifted back to

Paulette. It was so different from home, so removed. A few hours on the train and here they were, lifted into another world.

The desert swept away to the right and left of them. The mountains were ahead, although they would not ride that far today. This was to be a short jaunt. Later they would have the opportunity to ride farther if they wanted.

Everyone reined up on signal and dismounted. Canteens of cold water and paper cups were passed. It was getting warmer. The sun was climbing fast, round and hot. The air was dry. A brisk wind kicked up sand and the horses stamped, bridles jingling.

"Ooh, I love this!" Irma said with a grin. "I don't think I ever want to go home, Paulette."

"You ought to live out here, Irma," Mike said with his quiet drawl.

"Did you see that little band of Indians?" Irma asked. "Mike says there are several of them, just roaming around, pitching their tents here and there."

"I saw them," Paulette answered. "How do they earn a living?"

"Don't reckon they do," Mike replied, lifting his hat for a moment to let the air stir his curly brown hair. "They just drift. Get by the best they can."

The call came to saddle up. Everyone started back to their horses. Women were laughing and shouting at their clumsiness and one small girl in the group drew a toy pistol and fired it. Suddenly, Paulette was aware of a commotion. Whirling about in her saddle, she saw Boyd's horse rearing back on its hind legs. Boyd's face was angry and red as he suddenly slipped out of the saddle and was tossed to the ground.

Paulette was off her horse in a flash and running to him. Boyd sprawled on the ground, the wind momentarily knocked out of him. He sat up, rubbing his head. A small trace of blood was showing. The trail leader was there, bending over him. Mike had grabbed the horse and quieted him.

"You all right, mister?" the trail leader asked.

"Sure, sure," Boyd said angrily. "He just got scared and reared back. I wasn't prepared and the next thing I knew I was eating dirt."

"You struck your head against that rock," Paulette said. "Let me see the cut."

Boyd shook his head and got to his feet, disdainfully ignoring the hands that stretched out to help him.

"I'm all right. Let's get on with the ride. Sorry, folks; the show is over."

There was a ripple of nervous laughter, and finally everyone remounted and once again they were ready to ride. Boyd rode beside Paulette and continued to talk much as he had before. They turned around and headed back to the hotel. It was getting hotter. Boyd dabbed at his forehead with a handkerchief. The small cut had stopped bleeding long ago but Paulette could see the ugly dark purple of a bruise starting to show. Boyd looked white and strained under his hat.

"Boyd, are you certain you're all right?" she asked anxiously. "You took quite a jolt—"

They were nearing the stables. Paulette was glad of it. She was worried about Boyd. But he gave her a thin smile.

"I'm okay, I tell you! I'd much rather you'd stop being a nurse and just be the beautiful girl you are."

They had reached the stables. Mike was inviting Irma to lunch and Irma accepted. Paulette wondered what she would do with the rest of her day.

"I'll take your horse, miss," a stablehand said.

She was dismounting when she heard Boyd give a kind of groan. With alarm, she saw him slump in the saddle.

"Help me," Paulette called. "Someone help me. He's going to fall."

Mike came running. He got there just in time to catch Boyd as he toppled out of his saddle. Irma screamed. Paulette knelt beside him for a moment, taking his pulse and checking his color.

"Get some men to help you, Mike. We've got to get him inside to the doctor's office!"

V

As in all accidents, people senselessly crowded around Boyd for a look.

"Irma, keep them away," Paulette ordered. "Give Boyd air. Mike, see if you can find a stretcher—anything to support him while he's being carried."

"I've got a canvas cot," one of the stablehands said. "Would that do?"

"That would do fine," Paulette nodded.

The man went scurrying to bring it. Boyd was out cold. Paulette gently examined the bruise on the side of his head. It didn't look like much more than that, and yet it had caused this.

The men were back with the cot. Mike grabbed Boyd by the legs.

"Easy, fellas," Paulette cautioned. "Keep him as straight as possible as you lift him. It's important in case of head injuries."

They lifted him gently and firmly and Paulette nodded her approval. They started toward the hotel and Paulette fell in step beside them. Irma pranced along on the other side of the cot, looking frightened.

"Golly, Paulette, I didn't think he was hurt that much."

"Neither did I," Paulette replied. "But you never know in head injuries."

Word was passing rapidly as to what had happened. They were met shortly by the assistant manager of the hotel.

"Please, don't take him in the front way. The side entrance will do nicely."

"It's hot," Paulette replied. "And we've got a sick man. It's important to get him to the doctor's office immediately!"

The assistant manager rubbed his hands nervously. "Yes, yes, I understand. But I'm sure you understand my position too. We don't want to stir up any more excitement than necessary, now do we, miss?"

Paulette exchanged an angry glance with Mike, who shrugged his shoulders.

"Accidents give the hotel a bad name," Mike said in a low voice. "I reckon it's his job, Paulette."

"All right," Paulette said with a cold voice. "The side entrance."

Despite their cautious entrance into the hotel, the make-shift stretcher and the man that lay unconscious upon it were seen by many. The door that read *Doctor Ross Lane* was closed. Irma rushed ahead to open it. It was Paulette's first view of the office and it, like the rest of the hotel, was plush. The waiting room was well furnished and looked much like the lobby. The desk, normally occupied by the nurse, was empty.

Paulette moved to the inner door and knocked.

"Yes, who is it?" Doctor Lane called out.

"Paulette Castle. I've got an emergency for you. Could you see us right away?"

She heard his rapid footsteps and then the door opened. Doctor Lane wore a white coat and a bright tie. Apparently these were his regular office hours, what few he was required to keep at the Desert Plaza. His eyes quickly took in Boyd Sheridan on the canvas cot.

"Where do you want him, Doc?" Mike asked.

He looked at Paulette for a brief rundown and she told him all she could.

Shaking his head, he ordered them not to move him. "I'll check him right here first. Everybody out except Miss Castle."

Doctor Lane unbuttoned Boyd's shirt and listened with his

stethoscope. He peered under Boyd's eyelids and examined the bruise on the side of his head.

"Better call the ambulance again, Miss Castle. This man will have to be hospitalized. We'll need X-rays. I don't think there are any fractures, but we'll have to be certain. Probably a mild concussion."

Paulette got busy on the phone. She knew she should be used to emergencies like this, but her hand was trembling as she hung up the receiver. Was there intracranial bleeding? If so, surgery would be necessary. Was the small hospital at Sweet Springs equipped for that sort of work? A dozen questions raced through her head. Lying like this, Boyd Sheridan seemed so helpless, so completely different from the bold, strong man she had sensed him to be. But illness had a way of reducing everyone to a common denominator.

Paulette stepped outside for a moment to tell the few people still waiting what was being done. Irma twisted her hands together, tears glittering in her eyes.

"Gee, Paulette. What a rotten thing to have happen!"

"They'll take good care of him at Sweet Springs," Mike said confidently. "Come on now, I'll buy you something cool to drink."

Irma looked questioningly at Paulette. Paulette gave her a grin and a little push.

"Go on. I'll see Boyd into the hospital. It's the least I can do. Have fun. I'll see you later."

"You're sure it's okay?" Irma asked.

"Of course."

Mike took Irma's arm and led her away, his brown, curly head close to hers, talking in his quiet voice. By the time they disappeared down the hall, they were laughing together.

Doctor Lane stayed close to Boyd. Boyd hadn't moved or opened his eyes. In a short time, the ambulance came up the drive and Boyd was transferred to the ambulance stretcher.

"Going along?" Doctor Lane asked.

"I'd like to," Paulette replied.

"Glad to have the company. You can ride with me. They'll keep a close eye on Boyd."

For the second time, Paulette found herself climbing into Doctor Lane's modest convertible. They sped away from the hotel, where it shimmered in the hot sun. People were splashing in the pool and several, in swimsuits, were having lunch at the tables nearby, under the bright umbrellas.

"You're not having much of a vacation," Doctor Lane said with a smile.

Paulette turned her attention back to him.

"It's better than Bryson General Hospital. Besides, I've had a dip in the pool, attended a dance, and I went riding this morning. That's not so bad considering I've been here only a little over twenty-four hours."

"Your friend seems a lively sort."

"Irma is the salt of the earth. She's dreamed of this vacation for a long time."

"And you?" he asked.

"Me too."

"Somehow you don't seem the resort type, and believe me, I know all the types."

"It's a change of pace and a little luxury doesn't hurt once in awhile."

Doctor Lane smiled again. His thin face lit up and she wondered why he didn't do it more often.

"Somehow you don't seem the resort type either, Doctor Lane."

The smile was abruptly gone. A frown creased his forehead.

"I thought there weren't going to be any questions," he said.

"You're right. Sorry."

But she doubted whether she would be able to keep from asking them. There was much about Doctor Ross Lane that she didn't know and would wonder about until she had the answers. She was like that. There was a natural curiosity in her to know about people—who they were, what they wanted out of life, where they were going, and why.

Mostly, why. That was always the intriguing part.

They had reached the hospital. The emergency doors were open and Boyd was being wheeled in. She went with Doctor Lane to Admitting while he filled out the necessary forms. There were questions they had no answers for. But Boyd, once he regained consciousness, could tell the hospital what it had to know. Right now Boyd was being treated as an emergency, but not as anyone critically ill.

"By the way, how is our other patient, Mrs. Adams?" Paulette asked. "Did she have a good night?"

"Fair," Doctor Lane replied. "We finally reached her son. He's flying out today."

"Is she critical?"

"Possibly, Paulette. Right now it's a borderline thing."

"Would it be all right if I stopped in to see her?"

Surprise registered on Doctor Lane's face. "Would you want to?"

"Yes," Paulette replied. "Shouldn't I?"

Doctor Lane folded his arms across his white coat and grinned. "You only saw her very briefly last night. Yet you're interested, aren't you? Really interested."

"Of course!" Paulette exclaimed. "I'm sorry, Doctor Lane, but I'm not one of those nurses who regards patients as just a room number or a chart in the chart rack. They're people, real people—"

"And you like people," he said thoughtfully. "All kinds?"

"Of course, Doctor Lane."

"Ross. Call me Ross. Forgive the questions. It's just that too many professional people forget that it's human beings they're dealing with. They think in terms of statistics, facts and figures. They forget that behind it all is a smile, a beating heart, a laugh, a hand clasp—"

He broke off and laughed awkwardly. "Sorry. Let's see how Boyd's doing."

Boyd was just being lifted into his hospital bed from the stretcher. His eyes came open. Ross stepped up to him immediately and took his wrist to check his pulse.

"What's going on?" Boyd asked thickly. "Where am I?"

41

He tried to sit up in bed, but quickly clamped his hands to his skull and lay back down.

"Take it easy," Paulette said, bending over him. "That bump on the head was worse than you thought."

"You here?" he asked. "Is this the hospital?"

"Yes to both questions," she told him.

Doctor Lane reexamined him and asked several questions.

"What is it?" Boyd asked tiredly.

"Concussion. Probably not more than that, since you've regained consciousness. But we'll want to take tests and X-rays to be certain. It means a few days in bed at the best."

"Bed!"

"Bed," Ross said firmly.

He stepped out of the room and Boyd reached out to grasp Paulette's hand.

"What time is it?"

She looked at her watch and told him.

"I've got to make a call tonight. An important call."

"Sorry, Boyd. But there's no phone here. I'll see if I can get you one—"

"Yes. Do that."

Paulette stepped out to the desk and talked to one of the nurses on duty. She knew Boyd wasn't going to like what she learned. Going back into his room, he looked anxiously at her.

"Sorry, Boyd. There are no connections for phones in the rooms. This is a small hospital and—"

"No phones! Listen, I *have* to make a call. No later than ten o'clock tonight."

"There's a pay phone in the lobby, but you won't be allowed to use it, Boyd. Will you let me make the call for you?"

Boyd groaned and shook his head. "No. I've got to do it myself."

"Ah, secrets," Paulette teased lightly. "Who is she?"

"It's nothing like that!" Boyd snapped. "It's business. And very important!"

He was becoming much too upset. She tried to soothe him

and Boyd only grew more annoyed. Ross appeared in the doorway.

"What's going on here?" he wondered.

Paulette explained.

"She's right, Boyd," Ross said. "You've got to stay flat, at least until we know how things look inside your head."

"Well, let's get busy then," Boyd said angrily. "I've got to get out of here."

"The nurse will be in directly to take you to X-ray. Meanwhile, you're not doing yourself any good raging up a storm."

"Sure, sure," Boyd muttered.

"It will be a few hours before I get the results of the X-rays. There'll be some other tests too, Boyd. I'll see you again this evening."

"Okay," Boyd sighed.

"Are you certain there's nothing I can do for you?" Paulette asked.

"No. Thank you. Will you come again, Paulette?"

She smiled and nodded. "Sure thing. Be good and let the nurses take care of you."

She said goodbye and stepped out of the room. While Ross made a few additional notes on his chart, she went to see the stroke victim, Mrs. Adams. The woman remembered her. Her speech had been lost, at least momentarily, but she had the use of one hand. She stretched it toward Paulette and Paulette took it in a warm clasp.

"Hello, Mrs. Adams."

The woman smiled and Paulette said a few cheerful words to her, then left quickly. A long visit would only tire her, but Paulette was certain her short one had helped brighten her day.

"Ready?" Ross asked.

"Yes."

"This time I'll buy you lunch," he offered. "The Desert Plaza or somewhere here?"

"Anywhere," Paulette replied.

"I know a charming little place. Called *José's Diner,*" Ross laughed. "They serve good hamburgers."

"What are we waiting for?"

José's Diner was just what she expected—a small place with a counter and three booths. They specialized in Mexican food, but this time Paulette passed it by in favor of one of their super hamburgers.

Ross seemed at home here. She knew from the greeting he received that he came here often. Somehow José's Diner and the Desert Plaza didn't go together. It was one of the many questions that she had about Ross Lane.

"How long are you staying at the Plaza?" he asked.

"Ten days," she replied.

"Not very long."

"I'll be frank. On a nurse's pay it's as long as I could afford."

"Why here? Why not the mountains or Mexico or Canada?"

"Why not here? We thought we'd like the desert. We've never been here before," Paulette answered.

"I was born here," he said quietly.

She was surprised at the revelation. It was the first personal and direct thing he had said.

"At Sweet Springs?"

"No. Not really. In the mountains you see out of your suite at the hotel. In a small town there. A poor place. A lot of Indians live there. The poor devils—"

The compassion in his voice was a hot, angry thing.

"We saw some Indians this morning," Paulette said. "Someone said they were vagabonds, pitching their tents wherever they pleased—"

"There are small groups around like that. Everyone roars indignantly about the poor treatment of Negroes in the south. They should see how some of the Indians are forced to live."

"Can nothing be done?"

"You would think so, wouldn't you?" Ross asked angrily. "But there's almost nothing done!"

Their food arrived and Ross stopped talking about the Indians; in fact, he seemed to have forgotten them entirely.

When they had finished their meal, they climbed into his convertible and drove back over the hot highway to the Desert Plaza. Even now it looked like a mirage in the desert—cool, shaded, picturesque and carefree.

"It's ironic," he murmured. "Only a few miles away in the mountains there are the most impossible Indian slums you can imagine. Shacks—that's what they live in. The lucky ones, that is. I won't tell you what they have to eat sometimes. It would make you nauseated."

They walked into the hotel.

"I'll see you to your room," he said. "In fact, I think I'll catch a couple of winks."

The elevator door shut and he said nothing more. Then when they reached the third floor, he nodded curtly to the elevator boy, took her arm, and walked with her down the hall.

Paulette groped in her purse for her key and he took it from her fingers. The door swung open. Unasked, he stepped inside for a moment, leaving the door ajar behind him. The room was quiet. Irma was still out somewhere with Mike Allan.

"Paulette—"

He reached for her. She found herself suddenly engulfed in his arms, his thin, dark face hovering above hers. He was going to kiss her and panic spread through her. No, she wasn't ready for that.

Deftly, she stepped back from him. His face was unreadable. She couldn't tell if he were angry or not. He simply turned on his heel, opened the door, and stalked away.

She pushed the door shut, her heart pounding. That had been close. Too close. She had stepped away on instinct, remembering Jim Owens. Now, she wondered in a musing sort of way what Ross Lane's kiss would have been like. The odd part of it was, she didn't know if it mattered or not. But that was why she had come to Desert Plaza—to see if she could come alive again. So far it would seem that she was failing the test miserably.

VI

PAULETTE'S ROOM was icy cool. Too cool. The bright sunshine, even though it was hot, called to her. She skinned out of the riding clothes she still wore and into her swimming suit. Putting on a robe and thongs, she took the stairs down to the pool.

The splash of water, the bright clear sky, and the happy shouts of people relaxing made a smile come to her face. Surely if she were ever to shake Jim Owens out of her system, she could do it here. She spied Irma and Mike Allan at the other end of the pool, but they were so busy talking, Paulette decided not to bother them. Instead she spread her beach towel out on the hot cement in a secluded place. After a quick dip in the cool water, she smoothed lotion on her skin, and stretched out for a soak in the sun.

There were red fire pictures before her eyes, even with her eyelids closed. The cement simmered beneath her. But the sun laid warm, soothing hands on her skin, and she sighed audibly. At that moment a drip of cool water splashed on her arm. She opened her eyes to see George Hinkle bending over her.

"Oh, hello," he said. "How's the redhead today? I missed you at lunch."

"I didn't eat at the hotel," Paulette said, trying not to be annoyed at the intrusion.

"Oh, yes. You and Doctor Lane were busy again. I must say, you get around, don't you, Miss Castle?"

"You didn't go riding today," Paulette pointed out.

George's smile froze. "Well, ha, ha, I'm not much of a rider. Never was. That sort of thing is for the dudes."

"Then I'm a dude," Paulette said firmly. "I loved every minute of it."

George was busy eyeing Mike Allan and Irma across the pool. Irma had seen Paulette when she came out of the water and waggled a finger at her, then promptly forgot her. Which was fine with Paulette. Irma had come for a good time and Mike seemed to be supplying it. But as for George Hinkle, Paulette devoutly wished he'd find some other girl to charm.

"That's very cozy over there," George frowned, nodding toward Irma.

"They seem to get along very well. Must be a match in the making."

George looked a little green at that. But it sped him on his way and Paulette was left to her peace and quiet. That had been a cruel thing to do. But why let George get his hopes up? Besides, with a man like George, nothing was ever serious for long. Irma wasn't looking for that. She was looking for something permanent and if she found it here at the Desert Plaza, more power to her. But Mike Allan? Paulette frowned at the thought. Irma was a deserving sort. She hoped Irma would have the good sense to keep Mike Allan at arm's length. Romances started at resort spots didn't always last, and there was something wrong about Mike Allan. He was carefree and pleasant. Too carefree perhaps. What was he doing here at the Desert Plaza? If Irma hitched her wagon to that old car he drove, she might be in for a rocky ride.

Paulette sighed. She always worried about Irma. They were good friends. If it hadn't been for Irma's understanding and good humor, those first few days after her break with Jim Owens would have been unbearable. She owed Irma a lot and she never intended to forget it.

"She looks just too lazy," a voice drawled. "Yes sir, just too lazy. A dip in the pool is just what she needs!"

Paulette opened her eyes again. Mike Allan and Irma stood over her. The next thing she knew, Mike was picking her up in his arms. Then, with a swinging motion, he tossed her into the pool. Paulette shrieked and Irma's laughter rang out. Sputtering, Paulette came up, shaking her head. Mike was standing at the edge of the pool, holding his sides with laughter.

"Irma!" Paulette called. "Irma—"

She motioned wildly and Irma grinned. With a well-placed push, Mike found himself being shoved into the water too. Irma dived in and the three of them made a circle, laughing.

"Why is it nobody will let me rest?" Paulette asked.

"Who wants to rest?" Mike said, eyes twinkling. "You're here on vacation. Live a little, gal."

"You're doing enough of that for the three of us," Paulette shot back.

Mike's eyes sobered for a minute. "Yes, ma'am, I reckon I am. Why not? I always figure a day is just what you make it. And I aim to make it just as much fun as possible."

They emerged from the pool, dripping. The sun was beginning to fade. Swimmers were going inside.

"I think I'll have a nap in my room," Paulette decided. "Coming, Irma?"

"Sure."

"Ah, what for?" Mike asked. "Just because everyone runs inside about this time of day, doesn't mean you have to."

"We're having dinner together, aren't we?" Irma asked saucily. "What do you want me to do—wear a damp bathing suit into the dining room?"

Mike grinned. "Okay. Okay. You win. Paulette, you're going to join us. I won't take no for an answer."

"I'll see, Mike. Thanks for the invitation."

The girls hurried to their rooms. They flipped a coin to see who would use the bathroom first. Paulette won. The warm shower felt good and while Irma bathed, she did stretch out on the bed for a nap. But sleep wouldn't come. At home, plenty of times, she would have given anything for a few extra hours of sleep. But it was different here. There were no scheduled hours of work, no hectic rushing up and down the hospital corridors, no one calling in sick on the busiest day, no chewing out from a grumpy, overworked doctor, no killing pace that made skipping lunch necessary three days out of five. She was on vacation and perhaps Mike had a point. She should live a little.

They dressed for dinner. Mike picked them up promptly at seven. The dining room was busy but Mike was lucky. He drew a good waiter, and a very attentive one. He ordered for them and Paulette knew it was the most expensive item on the menu.

"Mike, you shouldn't spend all your money on us," Paulette protested.

"Money?" Mike grinned. "What's that suff?"

Paulette bit her tongue to keep from saying any more. It was obvious that Mike didn't have money to spend foolishly, but he was doing it anyway. His clothes were neat enough and well pressed, but they were not expensive. In fact they were very inexpensive. Paulette knew that in one glance. And the denims and boots he wore in the daytime were old and shabby. His car was a fright. How on earth had he scraped together enough cash to come here? Was he, like they, on a single blast? A spree?

The food was good. Mike talked quite a lot, but pleasantly, and he had a way of listening to what they said in return, as if he was storing it all away. Now and then there was a gleam in Mike's eye that didn't go with the rest of his character, but the gleam was always short lived, and after a time Paulette wasn't even certain she had seen it at all.

The evening was an enjoyable one. Paulette tried vainly to leave Irma and Mike alone, but neither would hear of it. Mike danced with both of them and told funny stories that made them laugh until the tears came.

They ended the evening early. At their door, Paulette moved away to let Mike and Irma say goodnight privately. After a moment or two, the door closed and Irma appeared, kicking off her shoes as she came.

"Well, that's that," Irma grinned. "Have fun?"

"Yes. But I felt like an intruder."

"Don't be silly. I wanted you there. Mike's sort of giving me the rush, kiddo, and I'm just not sure how I feel about that. With you around, he has to slow down a little."

Paulette laughed. "I see. So I was being used."

"Do you mind?"

"Of course not, silly."

"Where was the good doctor?"

"I haven't the slightest idea," Paulette frowned.

"I thought I detected a spark between you two," Irma pointed out. "Or is my radar clear off the beam?"

"There's no signal going out, Irma," Paulette sighed. "At least, not yet."

Irma bounced on the bed a couple of times. "Well, that's encouraging. You sound as if there might be. That's more like it, Paulette."

They went to bed, talking for a long time in the darkness before Irma fell asleep. Paulette didn't go to sleep so easily. She wondered about Boyd Sheridan. Ross must have phoned the hospital for the results of some of the tests. If she had looked him up this evening, she might have found out about Boyd. But she hadn't. Somehow she hadn't wanted to see Ross Lane again so soon, not after that brief scene at her door this afternoon.

In the morning the girls decided to have breakfast served in their room.

"Let's feel like queens for a change," Irma grinned.

"Live it up," Paulette smiled. "Mike's style."

Irma shrugged and picked up the phone to ask for room service. By the time they had dressed, the cart was at their door. The food was delicious and they ate on the balcony, viewing the spectacular scenery.

Paulette was on her last cup of coffee when there was a knock at the door. Irma, expecting Mike, went to answer it. But it was Ross Lane who stood there, black bag in his hand.

"I'd like to see Paulette, please."

Paulette left the balcony and said a cheerful good morning.

"I'm on my way to the Sweet Springs hospital. I thought you might like to come along and check on your friend, Boyd."

"I would. Thank you. I'll only be a minute."

The drive was a silent one after the usual comments on the weather. The hospital, though, was bustling. They found Boyd in a bad temper.

"I tell you, I am perfectly all right," he bellowed. "I want out of here."

"I have the results of your tests, Boyd," Doctor Lane said smoothly. "It looks like at least five days of bed rest for you. However, the concussion appears to be a mild one. No fracture."

"I tell you, I feel fine."

"I don't see you turning any somersaults," Paulette laughed. "Oh, come on, Boyd. Be a good sport. I'm sure Doctor Lane is only trying to take good care of you."

"Okay," Boyd said impatiently. "So, okay! But if I have to stay in bed, why can't I stay in bed at the hotel? At least I could have use of a phone there!"

"I'm not sure that's a wise idea," Doctor Lane said thoughtfully.

"Look, you're supposed to look after the hotel guests. Well, I'm a guest. If I need you, I'll phone. Room service can bring my meals. Now come on, Doctor, be reasonable!"

"I'll give it some thought," Doctor Lane replied.

He left the room and Paulette moved over to the window. Boyd stirred restlessly in bed. He did indeed seem able to leave the hospital, although she could understand Doctor Lane's caution.

"Paulette—"

She turned to face Boyd with a warm smile. He looked rumpled and disgruntled. His sort of man never took kindly to illness and he was no exception. Boyd Sheridan liked to be on the move.

"Did I catch a glimmer between you two?" he asked in

an angry voice. "You didn't really come to see me, did you? You came to be with him."

The accusation caught her completely off guard. What could it possibly matter to him, one way or the other?

"Aren't you being a wee bit presumptuous?" she asked.

"Am I? I liked your style the minute I saw you, Paulette Castle, and whether you know it or not I staked you out as mine."

"Maybe you just thought you did," Paulette replied, the heat coming up into her voice.

"The first night at the Plaza I asked you for a date and got turned down cold. Then what do I see? You and the doctor heading for the dance floor. I saw him step into your room too—for that sweet, sweet goodnight—"

"That's enough!" Paulette said, fists knotted. "You're being impossible!"

She moved with hard steps toward the door.

"Hey, wait!" Boyd called. "Wait—"

"I leave you in the hands of Doctor Lane and the hospital nurses. Good day, Mr. Sheridan!"

She would have slammed the door except for the general rule of quiet that always prevailed over a hospital. She was trembling with rage. She couldn't remember when she had been so angry. Just who did Boyd Sheridan think he was?

She went downstairs, found a snack bar, and ordered coffee. Sipping it, she forced herself to calm down. Doctor Lane appeared and climbed up on a stool beside her.

"I decided to let him go. He'd have this place in an uproar if I didn't. As for the hotel . . . well, they're trained to cope with all sorts," Ross said with a grin. "Although I'm sure the manager will rue the day he let Boyd Sheridan have a room. I'll have a bellboy assigned to stay near."

"He's insufferable," Paulette replied.

Ross' eyebrows went up. "I take it there was some sort of quarrel. He wouldn't tell me the details but I understand you walked out on him."

"I find his ideas quite crude," Paulette answered. "Do we have to talk about him?"

"Most certainly not. I've completed rounds. Mrs. Adams' son arrived and he's with her now. There's nothing more for me to do here. This time we'll have lunch in a proper place. At the Plaza dining room."

"Isn't this getting to be a habit?"

Ross looked at her with his dark eyes and nodded. "It is. I rather like it. But Boyd will probably have my hide for it when he's fit."

They laughed at that. Leaving the hospital, Paulette found herself looking forward to the lunch. Ross was pleasant company even though there were a lot of things she didn't know about him. Perhaps he would tell her something about himself today.

They were early for lunch. Mike and Irma were nowhere in sight. Only a few of the guests were in the dining room, one of them George Hinkle. He kept staring at them.

"I wish he'd just mind his own business," Ross said with annoyance.

"I know what you mean," Paulette smiled. "We hadn't been in the hotel an hour before we met George Hinkle."

"He keeps pestering me. Claims he knows me from somewhere else," Ross said. "I can't remember ever laying eyes on him before I came to the Desert Plaza."

They were halfway through their salads when George began to tablehop. He paused at each table to talk to anyone who would listen and busily told his stale jokes and his idle gossip. It was inevitable that he would also stop at their table. He sat down without being invited and inquired at length as to Boyd Sheridan's condition.

"I understand he's coming back to the hotel," George said.

"Any moment," Ross said stiffly.

George drummed the table top with restless fingers and smiled at them, the gold flashing in his teeth.

"Doctor Ross Lane. I swear I should remember you, Doctor."

"Sorry," Ross said.

Paulette busied herself with her salad, feeling Ross' anger

building by the second. George could be trying, but it was hard to figure why Ross was getting this angry.

George finally rose to go, having pumped all the information out of Ross he could about Boyd Sheridan, which was precious little. But Paulette knew George would busily spread this bit of news around the whole hotel.

George had gone. Ross heaved a sigh. "Thank goodness. It's hard to remember my good manners around that man. He absolutely provokes me!"

"Why?" Paulette asked.

The question slipped out before she could think about it. Ross' eyes held a guarded look. Then abruptly, George was back again, leaning both palms on the table top, his face glowing.

"By golly, I remember now! It just came to me. You were the fella. Yes, you were! The fella that was going around with Judith Arnold. I met you once at a party in New York. Remember?"

Ross had dropped his fork. He half rose out of his chair and then sank back again. Paulette saw a mixture of emotions flash over his face—surprise, indignation, anger and bewilderment.

"Sorry. I believe you're mistaken, George."

"No, I'm not. I'm not—"

"George, I believe that bellhop is looking for you," Ross said. "He beckoned—"

George straightened, stared, muttered to himself and hurried away. Ross was sheet white. He crumpled a cracker in his fingers and his jaw was set hard and tight.

"Ross—"

"The blundering idiot! Can't he leave a man in peace?"

Paulette said no more. What could she say? Ross had denied knowing Judith Arnold but Paulette was certain he did know her. Why would he choose to lie about it? Would all the questions about this man ever be answered?

VII

THE REMAINDER of their lunch together was uneasy and strained. Ross tried hard to gloss over the scene with George Hinkle, but he never quite succeeded. It was almost with a sense of relief that he took the check and said he had to get back to his office.

"Will Boyd Sheridan be okay?" Paulette asked.

"If he behaves himself. If he doesn't, I'll ship him right back to the hospital. I think I heard the ambulance pull into the drive just now. I'd better see him to his room. Want to come along?"

Paulette shook her head. She was still too angry with Boyd. Maybe that was a foolish attitude, considering that he was sick, but she did not like arrogant men and she never had. It was apparent that Boyd was a man of some position and perhaps used to having his own way, but she resented his behavior toward her.

Paulette went to her room. There was a variety of activities to choose from. There was always the pool. Bridge games were usually held in one of the clubrooms, there were horses to ride, tennis to play, or badminton, and in Sweet Springs there was a bowling alley, a theater, and shops catering to the tourist. A hotel limousine departed for Sweet Springs every hour. For that matter she could visit the reducing salon and see about taking off a pound or two while she was here. Not that she was really overweight, but no girl in her right mind would turn down an opportunity like that.

It was the pool that won out. She knew it would. From way back she was a lover of the sunshine. She stretched out on her beach towel and soaked for nearly an hour. No one bothered her. For once George Hinkle was absent, and even Irma and Mike Allan were nowhere to be seen.

Suddenly she was lonely. Snatching up her towel, she went back inside. As she passed the doctor's office, she caught a glimpse of Doctor Lane on the phone through the open door. He looked up, saw her, and beckoned.

With a sigh, Paulette went inside. It probably meant getting involved again. Some vacation! But she might as well admit it: ten minutes ago she was feeling bored. If Ross Lane could help her fill in an hour or two, why not?

He hung up the receiver with a frown. "That was the hospital. It's Mrs. Adams. Taking a turn for the worse. I've got to get there right away. I've been so busy, I haven't had a chance to do much more than see Boyd Sheridan to his room. He's been phoning. I haven't had time to assign a bellboy to help him. I'm sure he's all right, but would you mind—"

Paulette drew a long sigh. "Look, Ross, I'll take care of any of the other guests, do anything else to help you, but Boyd Sheridan—"

Ross grinned. His smile always caught her off guard. It was a very winning sort of smile, the sort that weakened women, charmed children and the old, and made almost anyone want to do as he asked.

"I thought you liked people," he pointed out. "All people."

He had flung her words right back into her face. She had to laugh. "You're right. You're reminding me that a good nurse doesn't discriminate between patients."

"Good girl," Ross aid, snatching up his bag. "Sorry I have to keep bothering you."

Doctor Lane hurried away. With a sigh, Paulette went back to her room, quickly changed into a cool dress and white, high-heeled slippers, and then went to knock lightly at Boyd Sheridan's door.

"That you, Doc? For crying out loud, come in! Don't just stand there!"

"Temper, temper," Paulette said as she went in.

He looked startled to see her. Then he grinned. "Well! My little angel of mercy."

"Let's get one thing straight, Boyd," Paulette said firmly. "I'm here at Doctor Lane's request. For no other reason. I'm to see that you're comfortable, find out if you need anything, and settle you until he gets back."

"Where is he? You mean the doctor isn't in the hotel? What if I need him?"

"You're doing fine. The woman at the hospital is very ill; she may be dying." She looked at him firmly. "Have you had any lunch?"

"No. I haven't had time to phone room service."

"Let me—"

"No!" he bellowed. "I'm expecting an important call any minute. I can't have my line tied up."

Paulette went to open the draperies and let a little sunlight in. "You'd rather starve than miss a call?"

"It's an important call," Boyd said stubbornly. "There should be a package of mints in one of my coat pockets in the closet. Bring it to me, will you?"

"For lunch?" Paulette asked with raised eyebrows. "Nothing doing. I'll phone from my room. What would you like to eat?"

Boyd stared at her. "I thought you were sore at me."

"At the moment I'm just your nurse, Boyd. Here at Doctor Lane's request. Now, what would you like to eat?"

"I don't care," he replied angrily. "I just want to get out of this stupid bed and get about my business!"

Paulette took a deep breath. "Mr. Sheridan, you're trying my patience!"

"Okay, okay. Order anything. I don't care. A sandwich will do. A piece of pie. Some coffee."

Paulette walked away swiftly, glad to get out of the room. The next time Ross asked her to look in on this man, she would flatly refuse, no matter how guilty he made her feel. After all, she was on vacation, wasn't she?

Room service was prompt. When the cart was wheeled into Boyd's room, she took over. With a couple of pillows propped behind him, he sat up long enough to munch the sandwich. But mostly he kept his eyes on the phone, as if willing it to ring. He ate hungrily enough and kept the food down. It was a good sign. When she started to remove the pillows, he protested.

"I like it better sitting up."

"The doctor doesn't," she reminded him. "You'd better stay quiet and flat, Boyd."

"I thought a bellboy was supposed to stay with me. Where in thunder is he?"

"I don't know. I'll call the desk if you want."

"Not on my phone!" Boyd shouted as she reached for the instrument. "How many times do I have to tell you? I'm expecting a call. My old man was out but I left word for him to phone back."

"Your father?" Paulette asked absently. "That's right, you're in business together."

Boyd sighed. "Together? Not really. I do the leg work, he makes the decisions."

Paulette studied Boyd's handsome face. He sounded irritated and angry. All was not well between him and his father.

"If you don't like it, why don't you quit?" she asked.

Boyd turned hot, angry eyes toward her. "You make it sound simple. Like a snap of the fingers."

"You're over twenty-one. You're able to make your own decisions, aren't you?"

His face worked. He didn't know whether to be angry or not. Perhaps she had hit a sore point. Somehow she wished she hadn't said anything at all. It didn't matter in the least to her what Boyd Sheridan did.

"If you need nothing else, Boyd, I'll leave you now," she told him. "I'll take the lunch cart out into the hall."

"Don't go," he said quickly. "Please, Paulette, don't go. Look, I guess I sounded off this morning at the hospital. I shouldn't have. I know that now. Stay awhile."

She shook her head. "You need a nap. If you need anything, live dangerously and use the phone for a couple of minutes. I'll be somewhere around the hotel. Doctor Lane will probably be back shortly too."

She opened the door. He began to yell protests at her leaving, but she turned a deaf ear to them. He was comfortable. He'd been fed and he was in bed as he was supposed to be. He could wait for his call in privacy.

Returning to her room, she found Irma there, looking sunburned, tired, and happy. Flashing a grin, Irma whirled around the room in a little dance.

"This is the best vacation ever, Paulette! I'm having so much fun!" Then her face sobered. "But you're not, are you?"

"Of course I am," Paulette said. "It's nice just not to be at Bryson General."

"But you've never really left the hospital behind," Irma protested. "You've been helping that good-looking doctor—"

"I'm sure his regular nurse will be back soon. Then I'll be free as a bird."

"Tell him you won't be available tomorrow. I've already made plans for us."

"And they include Mike Allan," she laughed.

"They do. There's a ghost town up in the mountains. He's going to take us there. We'll be gone all day. He said he'd have the hotel pack us a lunch and he's already spoken for our horses at the stable."

"Really, Irma, maybe I shouldn't—"

"Oh, but it will be fun!" Irma protested quickly. "I want you to come. Please."

The idea did sound like fun. She would be a fool to turn it down. Besides, she wanted to know this Mike Allan a little better.

"All right, Irma. You sold me!"

"Swell!"

"Irma, what do you know about Mike?"

Irma frowned and wrinkled her pug nose. "Not much by your standards. But I know I like him. He's fun. Never a dull moment. And he's easy to talk to. I like that. He's . . . well . . . Oh heck, Paulette, I might as well confess. I'm nuts about him."

"In such a short time?"

Irma picked up a hair brush and began to brush her hair vigorously. "I know what you're driving at. When I leave here, he'll forget me. That's what you mean, isn't it?"

"Partly. But you said something about him the other day. You said you could find his sort at home. So why the big attraction?"

"I don't know," Irma sighed. "Maybe I'm losing my good sense. Look, I'm not stupid and I'm not blind. I know he's extravagant. He spends money like he really had it. But I know he doesn't have anything really. Why, he doesn't even hold a steady job—just sort of drifts around. He told me that much. He's worked on all the big ranches in the state. He even rode with a rodeo for awhile. Stuff like that—"

"Do you think he's good husband material?" Paulette asked gently.

Irma made another face. "No! I know he isn't."

"But you're falling in love with him anyway?"

Irma nodded her head and flung her hairbrush aside angrily. "Yes, darn it, I am. I always said I would never marry an easy-come, easy-go type of guy. My mother did that, you know. Half the time we didn't even know where my father was. Mike would probably be just like that. Oh, Paulette, what am I going to do?"

"You could stop seeing him."

"How? The hotel isn't that big. Besides, he is fun—"

Paulette laughed. "Then it looks like you'll have to suffer the consequences."

The phone rang. Irma shook her head, indicating the call wouldn't be for her. With a frown, Paulette picked it up.

"Hello."

"Paulette," a voice gasped. "Please, come. I need you."

"Boyd, is that you? Boyd—"

The line had gone dead. She could hear a thumping sound, as though he had dropped the receiver and it was swinging, hitting a leg of the telephone stand. She slammed down the receiver.

"Irma, come with me," she said. "Boyd's in some sort of trouble."

They raced out of their room, not bothering with the elevator but racing up the stairs to the fifth floor. Pushing open the door, Paulette froze in her tracks. Irma let out a surprised little scream. Boyd was sprawled on the floor.

Paulette knelt beside him, trying her best to appear calm. Boyd was perspiring heavily and his face was chalk white.

She managed a faint smile. "What are you doing out of bed?"

"I thought I felt okay. You didn't get my mints out of my coat pocket and I decided I wanted them—"

Paulette took his pulse. It was steadying some now.

"I—I just blacked out," he said. "I came to on the floor. I managed to call you—"

"Okay," Paulette said. "Let's see if we can't get you back to bed. Irma, give me a hand."

It wasn't easy to help a man as big as Boyd back into bed, but Paulette was trained to do it the simplest way possible. In a few moments he was settled again. She bathed his face with a damp towel and he nodded gratefully.

"Feels good. I felt like a hundred sacks of cement had just been dumped on my head."

"You'll learn to mind the doctor," Irma said.

"Some people never learn though, do they?" he asked with a wry smile.

Paulette heard the wistful note in his voice. Right at this moment Boyd Sheridan was a very subdued young man. She checked his pulse and respiration and found them nearly normal again.

"You won't try that again, will you?" she asked.

"I still would like the mints. They're sort of a habit with me. Ever since I stopped smoking—"

Irma went to find them. He took the small package with a grin. "Everybody to his vice."

Paulette noticed Irma checking her watch. She probably had a date with Mike again.

"Run along, honey, if you want," Paulette said. "I'll stay with Boyd until Doctor Lane returns."

"Sure it's okay?"

"Of course," Paulette answered.

"Thanks a lot, Irma," Boyd said. "When they spring me from this place, I'll buy you the biggest steak you ever laid eyes on."

"That's a date," Irma grinned. Then with a wave of her hand and a kiss blown from her fingertips, she was gone.

Boyd grinned. "She's okay."

"She's very much okay," Paulette replied.

Boyd reached out and took Paulette's hand in his. "You too, Paulette. I knew that from the beginning. No, don't pull away. I won't get out of line again. But I mean it, Paulette. You're very much okay, too."

"Thank you."

He closed his eyes tiredly. "What brought you here? It wasn't just a vacation, was it? I've seen how you behave. You go away to yourself too much. You just lie in the sun and think. Even on the trail ride your mind was somewhere else."

"I didn't realize you were such an observing young man," she said as lightly as she could manage.

"It's my business to observe."

"Speaking of business, did your call come through?"

"Finally," Boyd answered. A shadow passed over his face. "It wasn't exactly pleasant."

"Didn't you explain about your accident?"

"No," he said. "My father doesn't like excuses of any kind. I don't want to talk about him, Paulette. I want to know about you. Why you look so sad sometimes."

Paulette looked away. Boyd's eyes studied her face. She could sense his gaze. It was sharp and analyzing, but not unkind.

"I lost someone," she said. "To another woman."

Boyd's mouth made the round shape of "oh" but the sound didn't come out. He squeezed her hand again.

"It will be okay, Paulette. Wait and see. It will be okay."

VIII

THE SKY WAS a fiery red in the east. The dining room had just opened, and Mike was waiting for them when they entered.

"Eat hearty, my girls," he said. "It will be a long ride into the mountains and to the ghost town."

"Was there once gold in the hills, Mike?" Paulette asked.

"Sure was. Gold Corners was the name of the town. Now there's nothing but desert lizards, tumbleweed and memories."

Irma shivered. "Sounds deliciously spooky."

Mike laughed. "Don't expect too much. But it's worth the ride. I always liked the tales of the Old West. Seeing a ghost town makes a man wonder what it used to be like there. In a way I wish I'd lived in those days."

Glancing at Mike, casually dressed in faded denims, scarred boots, and a stained Stetson lying on the floor at his feet, Paulette could believe it. This was a man who would have been a pioneer if he had lived then in the days of pioneers. He had the look about him of the outdoors—a rugged quality that was hidden by the flash of a warm smile —but there in the flinty gleam of his eyes was an expression now and then that held steel and strength. This was what surprised Paulette. It didn't match the rest of his easy-going character.

They ate a huge breakfast, more than they would ever have dreamed of eating at home. Mike devoured a steak and a side order of eggs, countless cups of coffee, and a stack of

63

toast. The waiter brought their lunch, neatly packed in a wicker basket, and they left the hotel.

The short walk to the stables was exhilarating after so much food. Their horses were ready. Mike saw them both mounted, strapped the basket of food and the canteens of water to his saddle horn, and then, with a wave of his arm and a yell that took one immediately into the dusty arena of a rodeo, they were on their way.

The sun was climbing steadily. The horses jogged along at an easy gait, and the rhythm of the swaying saddle threatened to put Paulette to sleep. But she couldn't get sleepy now. There was too much to see. The desert had to be seen to be believed. Such a barren country. Such a lonely place. She thought immediately of Jim Owens, and sighed. Lonely. Lonely. Lonely. Would it always be lonely for her without Jim? Or could this brief ten-day vacation help her forget him?

"Look!" Mike shouted.

A jet plane streaked through the sky, severing the blue with a white trail of vapor. A jet above, a horse beneath her. Paulette had to laugh.

"What's so funny?" Irma asked, squinting her eyes.

"What a difference in modes of transportation," Paulette replied.

"I prefer what we got," Mike spoke up. "Can't beat a good horse. He can take you places a jet can never take you."

"You own horses?" Paulette wondered.

"I've owned lots of them in my time," Mike replied smoothly. "I've sat on some devils too. I've got the busted ribs to show for it."

Paulette gnawed at her lip. Again there was no direct answer from him, nothing concrete. He said a lot but really told nothing. What was Irma getting into with this man? Why did he continue to be so evasive?

Perhaps it was only her imagination. It seemed everyone was evasive. Doctor Lane, Boyd Sheridan, Mike Allan. Perhaps it was only that in a place like the Desert Plaza people wanted to forget their identities, their troubles, and their ties.

After they had been riding for nearly an hour, Mike reined up and helped them dismount.

"We'll rest a bit. You dudes aren't used to long hours in the saddle."

"Don't underestimate us," Irma spoke up. "We got along real well on the ride the other morning."

"That wasn't a ride," Mike teased. "That was just to see how the saddle sat."

They rested on some rocks, shaded only by a tall saguaro cactus. The water from the canteen tasted faintly of aluminum, and Irma was already complaining of hunger pangs.

"Hungry!" Mike grinned. "You've a long time until noon."

They mounted up again and rode on. They were near the mountains now, and Mike assured them that it was an easy trail to the old ghost town.

As they rode into the foothills, Paulette spied a ragged tent of some vagabond Indians. Her heart turned over. A small girl stood there, staring at them with her round, dark eyes. She looked pathetically thin, her clothes hardly more than rags. She gazed at them with indifferent, perhaps frightened eyes.

"Poor thing," Irma murmured. "Mike, can't something be done for them?"

Mike shook his head. "Looks like it. Although to be truthful, they don't always want help. They're people of the open country, Irma. A roof over their heads stifles them."

Paulette listened. Mike spoke with authority. Then she remembered the raw compassion she had heard in Doctor Lane's voice when he had spoken of them. No doubt there were always two sides to any problem. But no matter what, there was no denying the swift, piercing sorrow in her heart, and the aching urge to do something for that little dark-eyed solemn Indian child guarding her pathetic home.

They pushed on. The mountains and the trail demanded all their attention now. The air was cleaner here—sharper, cooler. The mountains were rugged with scrawny brush, but a few pines mustered up out of the rocks, defiant and strong.

The higher they climbed, the greener it became. There was a stream here and there—a tiny trickle, but still water, fed from above where perhaps a few drifts of snow still remained.

They reached a summit and Mike once again reined up. Taking off his hat, he wiped his brow against his sleeve and grinned.

"Okay, girls, feast your eyes below. There it is—Gold Corners."

Paulette caught her breath. She had tried to imagine what it would look like. She had seen ghost towns in movies and pictures, but it was not like this. Nothing could capture the hot, scorching sun on the back of her neck, the parched white of the buildings, the lonely emptiness of a town that was no more. She saw the tumbleweeds pushed by the wind, heard the banging of a loose board, and could almost smell the hot, clean, sun-bleached wood and baked sand.

"Oh, I love it," Irma breathed happily. "It's—it's—"

Mike laughed softly. "I know. A thousand things crowd in on you at once. Who lived here? What were they like? How many men were killed on that street? How many were hanged? How many ounces of gold were freighted out of here? What ever happened to it? Is there gold still in the hills?"

He had said it all, almost eloquently. Mike might look like a saddle bum, but he wasn't. Paulette was certain of that now. But like the people who had passed here before them and gone, who was Mike Allan?

"Let's ride down. I know just the spot to have our picnic lunch," Mike said.

The ride down was not an easy one. The trail had changed. A rockslide had partially closed it. Mike led their horses over it and saw them safely into the town. An eerie feeling swept over Paulette. It was as though she were being lifted out of the present and dropped into a world of nearly a hundred years ago. Even the sight of a jet, should one appear now in the sky, couldn't shake this feeling.

They all felt it, and they grew quiet. Paulette spied a small graveyard where a wooden cross or two still stood. But the place had nearly been taken over by wild brush, weeds, and tumbleweed.

People had lived here and died. They had loved, hated, done business, gone to church, fought, prayed, cursed, and laughed.

"Oh, Mike," Irma sighed. "I can't describe it."

"How about our lunch over there?" Mike asked, pointing. "It was once called the *Red Star Saloon.*"

"How did you know?" Irma asked.

Mike laughed. "I used to make a study of ghost towns. Let's go inside."

The swinging doors were still there, at least one of them; the other had pulled free of it's hinges. Inside there was dust, sand, and cobwebs. Irma shrieked with fright as a lizard went wiggling out of sight.

The bar was intact. Mike pounded on it, making the dust fly.

"Set 'em up, bartender. Sarsaparilla for the ladies, Red-Eye for me—"

They started laughing. It broke the moody spell of the place. Finally they went to sit on the steps of the saloon, in a shaded spot, opened their picnic basket, and fell to hungrily. Never had food tasted so good. The lunch was a large one, ordered so by Mike, but they ate it all, down to the last crumb. Mike rationed the water carefully, leaving one canteen full to see them back to the hotel.

Mike's eyes busily scanned the area. He seemed to be enjoying the place as much as they.

"Have you been here often?" Paulette asked.

"Just once. Long time ago."

"You do get around," Paulette said lightly.

"That I do, Ma'am."

Mike still offered nothing about himself. Not really. If he had a home, he didn't tell them where it was. If he had a family, he didn't mention them. He was just a carefree guy on the loose and enjoying it. At least that was what he would have them think. Apparently Irma thought so. But Paulette wasn't so sure.

"Isn't there a legend?" Irma asked. "Usually there's some sort of story connected with these places."

"Sure there's a legend," Mike said. "See that graveyard over there? There's a young girl buried in it. Two men were going to have a gun battle in the street over her. When she heard about it, she rushed out to stop them and was killed by a stray bullet. Now they say the angels bless her and see to it that flowers always grow on her grave."

"Which grave?" Irma asked eagerly. "Mike, I want to see."

"The one next to the old fence. See that spot of color? That's it."

Irma was up and away. Paulette looked at Mike, and he winked. He had made up the story strictly for Irma's amusement.

"Mike, about you and Irma—"

The flicker was back in Mike's eyes again. He had sensed the serious purpose in her voice. Getting to his feet, he offered her his hand. "Irma's a cute kid. Come on. Let's look at the grave."

She went with him. What else could she do? Irma was on her hands and knees, pulling away weeds around the wild flowers that grew there. Paulette knelt down and straightened the wooden cross that had fallen over. With a small pile of rocks, she managed to keep it standing up. Perhaps it was just a made-up story about the girl, but it didn't matter. This was a nice gesture—the kind Irma would think of.

"There, that's better," Irma said, rocking back on her haunches and dusting her hands.

"Much better," Mike said. His voice was low and quiet. "You're quite a girl, Irma Wyse."

"Hadn't we better be starting back?" Paulette asked.

"You're right," Mike nodded. "Let's ride."

They left the old ghost town reluctantly. As they climbed up out of the valley, they paused again on the ridge for one last look. It was surely imagination, but Paulette was certain she could see the bright blooms of the wild flowers on the grave, nodding gently in the breeze.

The sun was high and hot, but the air in the mountains was cooler. With frequent rest stops, they made steady progress back toward the hotel.

It was nearly four o'clock when they reached the foothills. Paulette thought again of the Indian tent she had seen. Only a small child had been visible. Where were her parents? Had she brothers and sisters? What could they hope to find here in the foothills, and how did they manage to feed and care for themselves?

"Look!" Irma said, shouting. "There's that little Indian girl again."

Mike frowned and reined up. "She seems to want something. That's odd. Usually they stay clear of strangers."

"There must be something very much wrong," Paulette said. "Mike, we have to investigate."

"I suppose so," Mike answered. "Let me go."

"I'll go with you," Paulette insisted.

"Me too," Irma chimed in. "You're not going to leave me behind."

The three of them rode toward the girl. She was crying. Tears streaked her dirty face. Running toward them, she kept shouting incoherently.

Paulette dismounted. Kneeling beside the little girl, she touched her hand gently.

"Now, what is it, dear? Tell me, what's wrong?"

She kept pointing to the ragged tent.

"Johnny's sick. Real sick," she sobbed.

"Where are your parents?" Paulette asked.

"Gone."

Paulette stood up and started for the tent. Mike tried to stop her.

"You sure you want to mix into this?" he asked.

"Someone is sick in there, Mike. I have to."

Mike nodded. "Sure. You're right. We'll both have a look."

They left Irma to comfort the little girl and stepped into the ragged tent. On a pile of old blankets lay a small boy, a little older perhaps than the girl. He was feverish. Paulette could see that at once. She could see too that the child was seriously ill.

"Mike—"

"Tick fever," he said quickly. "I'm sure of it. It's no wonder, living in this filth!"

"Tick fever?"

"You've probably never seen a case of it, Paulette. But in the western states it crops up now and then."

"He needs help, Mike. Quickly."

"I'll talk to the girl."

Mike talked to her, managing to calm her down enough to learn in which direction her parents had gone. They had no pony. It wouldn't be hard to find them on horseback. He was about to mount up and start looking for them when the little girl broke away from them and ran. The parents were coming back. They stopped in surprise at the sight of three strangers by their tent.

Paulette listened while Mike talked to them.

"They don't want to let us take the boy," Mike said angrily. "They don't trust us!"

Paulette went to talk to them. "I'm a nurse," she explained. "I work in a hospital. There is a doctor at the hotel. He will see to it that your son is made well. This is very important."

"Do you want your son to die?" Mike asked impatiently. "He needs help."

The father shook his head. "No money," he said.

"Hang the money!" Mike snapped. "I'm Mike Allan. I'll see to it that the bills are paid. Let us take your son to the doctor at the hotel. You know the place."

"We know the place," the mother said tearfully.

"Bring your tent. Stay near the hotel. And let us take your son now."

They talked between themselves, looking first at Paulette and then at Mike. The mother crept away for another look at her sick son, and she must have seen that he was steadily growing worse.

"Yes. You take him," she said.

70

Paulette heaved a sigh of relief. "Thank God!"

Mike untied a slicker from his saddle. He went into the tent and in a moment came back with the boy bundled into it. Paulette held him until Mike was in the saddle. Then Mike took the boy into his arms and nudged his horse.

"Let's ride," he said. "The sooner we get there, the better."

Irma and Paulette needed no prodding; they were already mounted up. The boy was murmuring feverishly. Paulette sent one look over her shoulder and saw the Indian family already preparing to follow them.

"I'm surprised they trusted us," Paulette said.

Mike smiled. "The important thing is, they did."

"Mike, will he be all right?" Irma asked.

"I don't know," Mike answered. "Ask the nurse."

Paulette couldn't make a guess, even an educated one. She had never seen tick fever. But she did know the boy was very ill. She only hoped Ross could save him.

IX

IT SEEMED an impossibly long ride to the hotel. Mike pushed them along steadily, and twice they stopped to bathe the Indian boy's face with a handkerchief soaked in water from the canteen. Paulette moistened his lips too, and his fever-glazed eyes tried to smile at her. She was touched to the core—perhaps as she had never been touched before.

At last the hotel came into view. They ignored the stables and rode straight up the driveway to the front entrance. This would turn the assistant manager gray, but at the moment Paulette couldn't have cared less.

Opening the door, Paulette led the way to Doctor Lane's office. She was grateful to find it unlocked. Pushing inside, she found the waiting room empty. She knocked at the inner door, and Ross opened it with a scowl.

"I'm closed. Office hours have ended—" he began. Then he saw it was Paulette. "Oh, it's you."

"I've got another emergency," she said.

"You go out and drum up business, don't you? What is it this time?" he asked with a grin.

Mike carried the Indian boy into the examination room and laid him on the table. A deep frown and a flash of anger cut across Ross' face.

"What's this? What are you doing with an Indian here, Mike?"

"He's sick. I'll make a guess it's tick fever. We found him out in the foothills."

"Why here?" Ross asked in a cold, tight voice. "Why bring him here?"

Paulette was shocked at the grimness in Ross' voice.

"You were the nearest doctor, Ross. Please, the boy needs immediate attention," Paulette said.

"It was your idea to bring him here?" Ross asked, chin up, hard and tight.

"It was. Mike and Irma agreed. We have the parents' permission."

"I'll bet you do! They don't trust white people. Didn't you know that?"

"Maybe so," Mike said with his easy drawl. "But they seemed to trust me. Now, get with it, will you, Doc?"

Ross was outnumbered. Paulette was stunned that he hesitated even for a moment. There was some kind of inner turmoil in this man. It showed on his face. Then finally, with a wave of his arm, he motioned them out. Paulette didn't move.

"You too," he said.

"No," Paulette said stubbornly. "I promised this boy's mother I would stay close until he was cared for. I intend to do it."

"Well, since he's here there's nothing left to do but examine him. Help me strip off these filthy rags. There's clean linen in the closet. Bring a couple of sheets. We'll wrap him up in them."

"It will be the hospital for him, won't it?" Paulette asked.

"Yes. Mike's probably right. It looks like tick fever at first glance. God knows I've seen it many times. When I was a boy the Indians often had it."

Ross was quick and thorough with his examination. The boy's temperature was very high. He was irrational and complained of his head hurting. A rash had appeared on his body. He was so ill he was barely aware of where he was or that someone cared for him.

The ambulance came again. Since Paulette had arrived at the Desert Plaza it had come every day. By now it was getting to be a usual sight to see it come screeching up the drive.

As Paulette climbed into the ambulance with the sick boy, she glanced around, looking for his parents. But then, of course, it was too soon for them to have arrived. It would take them a long while on foot, dragging their belongings behind them on a kind of stretcher.

The hospital went into quick action. Tests were ordered; the boy was bathed and dressed in a hospital gown. Medications were started for his headache, and shortly Ross had the results of the tests from the lab.

"Tick fever," he nodded. "We'll begin antibiotics immediately."

"What are his chances?"

"Too soon to say," Ross replied. "But let's face it, Paulette. This boy is generally run down. Malnutrition. Look at those ribs showing, and how thin his arms and legs are."

"You do care, don't you?" she asked. "Back at the hotel—"

Ross whirled to face her, anger flashing over his face.

"What do I care about that—that little waif of humanity? Others have forgotten him. They don't always do what they should to help themselves. Many of the men drink—they can't resist whiskey. It makes them like mad dogs! What do I care?"

Ross was shaking with rage. Paulette was so startled, she could only stand there, stunned, as he slammed out of the hospital room. She heard his heels strike against the hall floor, hard and sharp.

Paulette went to look for him. He wasn't at the desk and he wasn't in the snack bar. There was a small chapel off the lobby, used for families of very sick persons, and she found him there, hunched over in a chair, head in his hands.

"Ross—"

He raised his head. "Go away."

"No," she said firmly. "You're a man talking in circles, and I don't understand you. The other day you were for the Indians; today you seem to talk the other way. You didn't even want to treat this boy—"

Ross laughed bitterly. "No. I didn't. But I have my reasons. And I don't want to discuss them with you."

Paulette straightened, hurt by the anger in his voice and his rejection of her.

"I didn't mean to intrude, Ross. Sorry. I'll see if I can catch the hotel limousine and go back to the Plaza. It doesn't seem that I'm needed here."

She thought he would call her back, but he didn't. She left him there, head in his hands, muttering to himself—a man torn by some indecision she couldn't begin to guess.

It was nearly dark now. It had been a long day and she was tired. The limousine usually deposited passengers and picked them up in front of the Blue Ridge Café. But when she reached the café, she learned she had just missed it. It meant an hour's wait until the next one came.

"Hello!"

She wanted desperately for the ground to open up and swallow her. She was never in the mood for George Hinkle, and tonight she was exhausted, worried about the Indian boy, and more than a little annoyed with Ross. But here was George Hinkle, grinning, the gold in his teeth showing. He pounced on her like she was a long-lost friend.

"You waiting for the hotel limousine too? It seems we just

74

missed it. That gives us an hour. Come along, beautiful; we'll have supper. The Blue Ridge serves a decent meal."

"Thank you, George, but I'm not dressed. I've been on a trail ride—"

"Nonsense. There isn't a thing wrong with you. Come along."

He took her arm and propelled her inside. The place was dimly lighted and she was glad of that. She felt hot and mussed. Most certainly she wasn't in the mood for dinner with George Hinkle.

He ordered for them with aplomb and made a few stale jokes to the waitress. She was a seasoned waitress, Paulette thought; she ignored his remarks with a stiff, tolerant smile.

"Now," George said, rubbing his hands gleefully. "Tell me what you've been doing today, Paulette."

So she told him about the Indian child she had helped bring to the hospital. George listened closely. He wanted to be certain he had all the details.

"A little out of Doctor Lane's league, isn't it?" George said with a sly smile.

"A doctor is a doctor," Paulette said, trying hard to hold her temper. "A doctor treats illness wherever he finds it."

"Still, it's not Doctor Lane's style. He caters to the rich old ladies at the hotel, or the young heiresses, or the millionaires who eat too much and get their ulcers in an uproar. Let's admit it, Paulette, darling—Doctor Lane has a very high-class clientele."

"Perhaps," Paulette said. "But that doesn't mean—"

She broke off. Why was she defending Ross? After what she had just seen at the hospital, how could she? Was George Hinkle right? Was Ross just a doctor for the bluebloods? Was that why he disliked the whole idea of the Indian child?

"He's always been for the social set, my dear," George said knowingly. "Judith Arnold is well known socially, and her father is one of the best-known surgeons in New York. Naturally Ross Lane moved in those circles."

"Judith Arnold?" Paulette asked.

"When Judith Arnold gives a party it takes a gold-engraved invitation to get in. I was invited there once. Just once! And I don't mind telling you, my dear, I've brushed elbows with the best of them. That's where I met Ross. As I remember it was getting to be quite the serious thing between those two. Ross was going to join forces with her father in a very lucrative practice."

Paulette struggled to keep a smile on her face. Not that this should upset her. What did it matter what Ross had planned to do with his future?

"Then what is he doing out here at the Desert Plaza?" Paulette asked.

George shrugged. "Search me. Maybe things aren't going so well between them now. Did you notice how white Ross got when I mentioned her name? And he pretended he didn't even know her—"

"It does seem strange," Paulette admitted. "Perhaps he just didn't want to discuss her."

George grinned. "Oh, come now. Any man would be delighted to say he even knew Judith Arnold, let alone be on a very friendly basis with her. She's a knockout, Paulette—a real gorgeous dish."

Their food came. For some reason Paulette wasn't the slightest bit hungry. She just wanted the hour to pass quickly so she could return to the hotel. George kept prattling on, but he had got off the subject of Ross and Judith Arnold. He was trying to impress her with a list of all the places he had been, the women he knew, and the things he'd done. George, in his own eyes, was irresistible to women. Poor George, Paulette thought. She heartily hoped no one ever punctured his bright balloon and told him that he was actually not much more than a bore!

At last she saw the limousine arrive and they left the café. All the way back to the hotel she had to listen to more of George's prattle, and once he tried to put his arm around her. With an icy smile, she took his arm away.

"Watch it, George. I'm not your type. Let's remember that, shall we?"

George gave a hollow laugh and stared out the window, finally out of words.

The hotel had never looked so good. Paulette went directly to her room, walking away swiftly from George.

Irma was out. There was a note propped on the pillow. She and Mike were going to Sweet Springs to a movie and to pay a quick visit to the Indian boy, Johnny.

Paulette was tired. Exhausted was a better word. She headed for a refreshing soak in the tub and decided to spend the evening in her room. There was always television and the neglected books she'd intended to read.

It wasn't late when someone knocked at her door. Pulling her negligee around her and thrusting her feet into high heeled mules, she went to see who it was.

"It's Ross. Let me in, will you?"

She opened the door. They exchanged a glance. His was tortured and uneasy. His dark eyes swept over her and there was a note of approval in what he saw. She blushed and wished she was dressed more appropriately.

"I have to talk to you."

He closed the door behind him. It seemed suddenly as if the walls were closing in on her. With a half desperate move, she went to the sliding doors, opened them, and stepped out to the balcony. He followed her. It was a clear, clean desert night. Off some distance she saw the flicker of something that looked like a fire.

"What's that?" she asked.

"The Indians. Parents of the boy," Ross said. "The hotel wouldn't let them pitch their tent any closer."

"Naturally not."

"They have their guests to think of."

"Of course," Paulette said coldly.

"What must you think of me?" he asked. He reached out and turned her toward him. "You must think I'm a fool or an idiot, the way I keep contradicting myself."

"I must say, I have my questions. But you made it plain from the beginning, Ross, that I wasn't to be curious about you. So I won't ask."

77

"But you no longer quite trust me, do you?"

"I never thought you would hesitate to care for a very sick little boy, Indian or not!"

Ross stiffened. His shoulders sagged for a moment.

"I had that coming. There's much you don't know about me, Paulette. And I'm not ready to tell you just yet. I want you to know I've done everything in my power for Johnny and I will continue to do so. I want to make him well, but I'm not at all sure I can."

"It isn't necessary for you to tell me this," she answered.

His hands tightened on her shoulders, his strong fingers making her wince. His dark face came closer.

"But it is, Paulette. Suddenly, tonight, I knew that. Paulette—"

He kissed her. She couldn't have stopped him if she had wanted to. The kiss was long and hungry, a burning kind of a kiss that a man gives a woman when he needs her especially much.

At last, she broke away from him. "Ross, please—"

"There's someone else, isn't there?"

"There used to be. That's why I'm here, to forget him."

His lips lifted in an ironic smile. "The Desert Plaza is just the place to sort out your heart. That's what I told myself when I took this job. I'm not sure that it is. I'm still just as mixed up, as confused, as uncertain—"

He stopped talking. His long fingers touched her cheek gently.

"Paulette—"

"You'd better go now. Please . . ."

"If I go now, I'll be back. Soon. If not tonight, tomorrow. If not tomorrow, the day after. Paulette, I have no right to offer my love to anyone, but right this minute—"

She moved away from him, her head and her heart spinning. Too much was happening, too soon. She wasn't ready for it. He followed her to the door. Before he opened it, he kissed her again—a cool, dispassionate kiss, but somehow it burned just as deeply and stirred her just as much as the other one.

Then very quietly, he opened the door and closed it behind him. The click of the latch was lost to her, drowned and smothered in the fierce pounding of her heart.

X

DOCTOR ROSS LANE moved away quickly from Paulette's door. He wasn't certain why he had gone there in the first place. Perhaps he felt he owed her an explanation. God knew he had been acting strangely enough. A flash of self-hate went through him. Why had he hesitated even for a moment when Paulette had brought in Johnny? Maybe part of it was the fact that it wasn't his job to take in Indian waifs and care for them. His job was with the hotel and their guests. Nothing more.

This was supposed to be one of those lucrative, soft jobs that a man dreamed of. There was plenty of free time, luxurious surroundings, interesting people, and seldom the kind of case that meant any challenge or real concern. These were people in transit, here for a few weeks, a month, maybe only a few days. He could forget them the moment they checked out, almost certain that he would never see them again. That was what he wanted, wasn't it? Nothing binding; no ties, no time to think or explore his own heart; no time to make a decision that would affect the remainder of his life.

He pressed the button for the elevator and stepped inside when the doors opened. Nodding curtly at the uniformed boy, he exchanged pleasantries with him. The people liked him here. They respected him. The pay was excellent. So why be in such a turmoil? Why not stay here indefinitely? Swim in the pool, go riding, dine on the best food—

The door opened and he stepped out. It was past office hours. That was another nice thing—his office was open only a few hours every week. Of course he was always on call. There were always minor accidents and illnesses. Sometimes there was something major, such as Mrs. Adams, but it wasn't the general rule. Sick people usually had the good sense to stay home and not go on vacations.

He unlocked the office door and stepped inside, flipping on the lights. The plush carpeting and deep, soft chairs, the indirect lighting—all of it jarred his nerves.

He went back to his private office. The room was cool. The air conditioning hummed. His head was aching, throbbing like a drum. He went to the medicine supply closet and took two aspirins. But aspirins weren't going to help the kind of headache he had. His ache stemmed from deep inside him and he knew it.

The phone rang. With a weary sigh, he answered it.

"Doc? For crying out loud, where have you been?"

"Busy, Boyd. How are you feeling?"

"Haven't you seen Paulette? Didn't she tell you? I passed out cold, Doc. Look, I want you to check me over again."

Ross straightened with alarm. Why should he have fainted?

"Boyd, did you get out of bed?"

"Yeah, yeah. Look I've been properly scolded for that already. You coming or not?"

He didn't want to see Boyd. There was probably no real need. But Boyd was a hotel guest and he was also a patient.

"I'll be right there, Boyd."

He took his bag and left the office. The elevator took him up to the fifth floor and he found his way to Boyd's room. Going inside, he saw Boyd glaring angrily at the ceiling.

"I want out of this bed, Doc," he began to yell. "I've got things to do."

"Calm down," Ross said with a grin. "What's that you're eating?"

"Mints. I'm about out of them. I'll have room service bring up some more."

"Mints?" Ross asked with raised eyebrows.

"Okay, so it's nuts, but they help me calm down."

"I don't think they're working this time," Ross laughed. "Let's have a look."

He checked Boyd thoroughly. Pulse and respiration good. His color was good too. There was no weakness in either arms or legs, and any fool could see that Boyd Sheridan was not drowsy. But then he had not expected to find any of these things, for the X-rays and tests at the Sweet Springs hospital had proved this to be only a mild concussion.

"How soon can I get up?" Boyd asked.

"Perhaps tomorrow you can try it for a few minutes. But only if I'm here or someone is with you."

"Like Paulette?" Boyd asked with a grin. "Say, she's an eyeful, isn't she?"

Ross felt the back of his neck grow warm. He knew Boyd was smitten with her. But he knew Boyd's type. When he walked into a hotel or a night club, he automatically looked around until he found the most attractive woman there and set her as his goal.

"It would have been best if you'd stayed in the hospital," Ross pointed out. "You would have had proper nursing care there."

Boyd grinned. "Maybe. But I wanted to come here."

"And you always get your own way?"

Boyd shrugged. "Not always. My old man—"

A shadow passed over Boyd's face.

"I take it you were able to make that important phone call," Ross said.

"Finally," Boyd replied with a scowl. "How soon tomorrow can I get up? In the morning?"

"We'll try it when I check you over. Okay?"

"When will that be?"

"I have a seriously ill patient at the hospital. I'll go there first. I'll get to you about ten probably."

"Ten!" Boyd complained. "Can't you make it sooner?"

Ross snapped his bag shut. "No. Sorry."

"You're a cool customer, aren't you?"

"Am I?" Ross asked with a slight smile. "Good evening, Mr. Sheridan."

Ross took his bag and walked out of the door, leaving Boyd sputtering behind him. He wished Mrs. Adams were feeling as spunky as Boyd. Poor Mrs. Adams. His emergency call to the hospital earlier had prepared him for the worst, and he had found it. If she lasted through the night, he would be surprised. But he could always hope. She had suffered a second stroke. If there was a third—

Ross sighed, aware of how tired he was. He shouldn't have gone near Paulette, feeling as he did. He was too vulnerable when tired. He let down too much, revealed too much.

He remembered vividly how she felt in his arms, the soft sweetness of her lips, and he was a little ashamed of the hunger in him he had let her see.

Hunger! Perhaps any woman would have served. But he rejected that idea immediately. He was tired, lonely, and his heart was rocking. All because of the Indian boy, Johnny, and the fact that around a small fire just a short distance from the hotel, camped on the desert, were Johnny's people.

Instead of returning to his office, he went to his room. Without turning on the lights, he stepped out to his balcony. All rooms had a balcony, and his looked west—just as Paulette's did. Was it possible to see the flickering Indian fire? Or was it only his imagination?

The phone rang.

"Doctor Lane," he answered.

"Ross!"

He froze. He knew that voice. Hadn't it haunted him for too long?

"Hello, Judith."

"It's been a long time."

"Has it?" he asked.

"Darling, why do you have to do such rash, impulsive things? Why couldn't you have listened to reason. I've been perfectly miserable ever since you left here—"

He tried to imagine how she looked at that moment. But the few months he had been here blurred his memory. It was just as well. She was so beautiful—so cool and beautiful. So persuasive. She made a man want to tie himself in knots for her. But the knots had stifled him, nearly cut off his blood supply for good. So he had come here, to get things straight in his own head.

"When are you coming home, darling?" Judith asked. "Daddy won't wait forever, you know."

"I didn't know he was still waiting!" Ross said with alarm. "Judith, I told you when I left I didn't think I'd want to be associated with him. I have my own plans—"

"He's waiting. I asked him to," Judith replied. "I was so certain you'd come to your senses."

"Oh, were you? Maybe I have come to my senses, for the first time."

"As a doctor in a resort hotel?" she scoffed. "Such a waste. Such a horrible waste. Daddy says—"

He clenched the phone tighter. He had all the respect in the world for Sam Arnold. He was a good doctor. A high priced one maybe, but still a good doctor. It mattered what Sam thought of him, but right now Sam Arnold had nothing to do with him.

"Judith—"

"It's those Indians, isn't it? You can't get those dirty Indians out of your mind!"

"Hang up, Judith. I won't listen to this."

"I'm coming out there. I want to talk to you."

"No!" he spoke harshly. "The minute you arrive, I'll leave. I mean it, Judith. Stop pushing, will you?"

"I won't wait forever, Ross. I let you run away to have time to yourself. I'm getting tired of explaining that my fiancee is practicing somewhere else. You belong here with me!"

"I never asked you to wait," Ross said stiffly.

"I thought you loved me," she said.

He closed his eyes against the warmth of her voice. She used her voice to melt him. She always had. Judith was not an easy woman to resist. When she held out her arms to him, he was a man in a dream, her prisoner. Coming here, he had escaped some of that. But it was still there, burned into his memory, and he felt it coming over the line now.

"I can't talk any longer, Judith," he said hastily. "Goodbye."

He hung up. Perspiration dotted his face, even in the cool room. It was the first he had heard from her since coming here six months ago. She had been biding her time, letting her silence work for her. More than once, he had reached for the phone to call her. More than once he had nearly thrown over everything and flown back to her, ready to take her father's offer, to lose himself in her nice, plush, comfortable world.

But he had stayed here. The desert and the mountains in the near distance had held him in a vise. He hadn't gone home. Not once had he let himself put a foot into that little mountain village called Rugged Rock. Because he had known what would happen—memories would flood into his heart, drown him. He would be hopelessly snagged and he knew it. He knew what it meant. There would be more agony than happiness there: lack of medicines, ignorance to fight, suspicion, no pay, long hours, impossible conditions—and no one to help him. This was the worst. He didn't think he could bear it alone.

Stepping out to the balcony again, he strained his eyes to see the tiny Indian fire burning in front of a ragged tent. Johnny's people—vagabonds. Restless, roaming people who owned nothing but their tent and the few meager belongings inside it. How did they live? How did they exist? If Paulette hadn't intervened, they would probably have a dead son by now. As it was, there was hope for him.

But for Dave there had been no hope. Ross' eyes burned. He and Dave had been boys together, their friendship sealed with the mingling of blood from slashed wrists. His blood had been that of a white man, Dave's that of an Indian.

Dave's Indian name was Deer In The Wind. He had known more about the outdoors than Ross had ever dreamed existed—how to track, how to find firewood, how to know the right spot to pitch a tent or to bed down. His sand paintings were a work of art. His laugh had been as free as the wind, his eyes dark and dancing. His heart had been strong and faithful and they were friends—for life.

Only Dave hadn't lived beyond his sixteenth year. When he grew suddenly ill, his people treated him with their own herbs and medicines. Ross had begged them to take him to the doctor in Sweet Springs, but they had not listened. They looked at him with their cold, hard eyes and he was no longer Dave's blood brother. He was a white man, interferring.

Dave died. On a cold, starlit night when the first flakes of snow fell, marking the winter, Dave died and something was born in Ross. He would become a doctor. He would be a good one. He would come back to Rugged Rock and he would take care of the Indians. He would not let others like Dave perish needlessly. He would avenge Dave's death in this way.

Well, he had become a doctor and a good one. But other things had come along, among them Judith Arnold. Judith, and her father, and an offer that a boy who had always been poor all his life found hard to turn down.

Still the mountains had called to him and the memory of Dave. They had torn at him, ripping him apart. Half of him wanted to stay with Judith; the other half had to come home.

So he had compromised with himself and come here, within sight of the mountains of home. He had forced himself to take a meaningless job at the Desert Plaza to give him time to decide.

Ross left the balcony and, not bothering with the elevator, walked from the hotel. He knew where he was going, and it wasn't far. Sand got in his shoes. His jacket felt too warm and there was a hard pounding inside his chest.

They heard him coming. They probably had heard him

several minutes before they saw him. They could sense things in the darkness that a white man would fall over.

They stood back from the fire that had nearly gone out now. The remains of their meager supper could be seen in a blackened pan resting in the coals. He didn't know them. For that much he was glad.

"I'm Doctor Lane," he said. "I'm caring for your son, Johnny. He's at the Sweet Springs Hospital and doing as well as can be expected."

"He'll get well?" the mother asked fearfully.

"I hope so," Doctor Lane said.

The father straightened. He was an ugly Indian—tall, weathered, and suspicious.

"He'd better get well, mister."

Ross swallowed. "He's a sick boy. You must have realized that. Why else did you let the nurse take him?"

"Allan said he'd pay," the father replied.

"Mike?" Ross asked.

But that was of little importance now. It was strange they had given Johnny up so easily. But that didn't matter now either. What worried Ross was the hard glint in the father's eye.

"If you want to visit him, I'll see to it that you get a ride to Sweet Springs," Ross offered.

"We'll go when we please," the father replied.

"All right. I'll be talking to you again."

"He'd better not die," the father said again. "You remember that."

XI

Ross Lane's kiss had upset Paulette more than she liked to admit. For a long time after he had gone she simply stood on the balcony and stared out into the desert night. Music drifted up to her. It was beautiful music, but it made her sad because it reminded her of Jim Owens. . . .

She knew abruptly that she didn't want to stay in this room another minute. Even if it meant being alone in a crowd, she still wanted to feel within touch of humanity.

Dressing quickly, she went downstairs. There was a dance every night. The Social Director, a swift walking, bright-eyed woman, swept down on her.

"Oh, hello there. Do come and join the dance. Isn't the music good tonight?"

Paulette smiled but the smile felt stiff. Nevertheless she let herself be taken along. Mike Allan saw her enter. He was on his feet in an instant and coming toward her.

"Hi," he said. "It's okay, ma'am. I'll take over from here on."

Paulette gave the Social Director an appreciative smile and she hurried away to spread her charm elsewhere.

"Don't tell me you're alone," Paulette said, feigning surprise.

Mike nodded. "Afraid so. Look."

George Hinkle had claimed Irma for his own and was whirling her about the dance floor, taking up enough room for three couples. Irma wore a pained, tight smile on her face. Poor Irma. Her toes would be tramped black and blue.

"Are you going to let George get away with that?" Paulette asked with surprise.

Mike smiled. "For a little while. Besides, this is just the

opportunity I've been waiting for. I'd like to talk to you, Paulette."

"Me?"

"Let's take a walk. Okay?"

Mike didn't give her a chance to protest. He took her arm and they wound their way through the crowd and into the lobby. They left by way of the side entrance. The pool was being used by a few night swimmers, but most of the hotel guests were dining or dancing.

Mike walked with the easy stride of a man who had all the time in the world. He was probably the most casual man Paulette had ever known.

He whistled a tune quietly and twisted his head to look up at the stars.

"No rain in sight. I wonder what the desert would look like if it had a decent annual rainfall. Think of the cattle a man could graze here."

"Are you a rancher, Mike?"

He laughed. "I thought I told you. I'm a Jack of all trades. I dabble in everything."

Evasiveness again! Paulette decided not to press the point. What was the need? In a few days their vacation would be over, and she and Irma would be heading back to Bryson. Bryson had been home for several years now, but she didn't really want to go back. But her work was there. Just because the memory of Jim Owens was there too, was no real reason for her to leave permanently.

"Paulette, you've been Irma's friend for a long time, haven't you?"

"So that's it," Paulette laughed. "You want to know all about Irma."

Mike shrugged self-consciously. "Well, yes, I do."

"What can I tell you? By now you must know Irma fairly well. It doesn't take long to know her—"

"She comes from a good family, doesn't she?"

"All but her father. He was too carefree, too irresponsible. Irma always said she wouldn't marry a man without roots. Deep-down roots."

Mike took off his hat and twirled it restlessly. "I suppose that lets me out."

Paulette was jarred. She knew there were sparks between these two. She even knew that Irma thought she was in love with him. But at the same time she had expected it to blow over once they had gone home. Now here was the same serious note in Mike's voice.

"Mike, are you in love with Irma? I mean, really in love?"

Mike laughed. "Well, now, ma'am, I sure do get a palpitating heart whenever I look at her."

"Love is more than a pounding heart, Mike," she said thoughtfully, but she was remembering her own pounding heart when Ross had kissed her.

"I know that," Mike said. "Man, how I know that! I don't mind telling you, I've been singed a few times. It makes me extra cautious."

"Irma is an open hearted, fun loving girl, Mike. We're good friends and we share confidences, but I can't speak for her. Not in matters of the heart. You'll have to ask Irma these things, not me."

"It's just that I want to be sure this time, Paulette. Really sure. I want to check out all the angles."

"If you mean, is Irma stringing you along, the answer is no. She's too honest for that. She genuinely enjoys your company, Mike. But there are doubts—"

"Doubts?" Mike asked, coming to a halt. "What sort of doubts?"

"You know. You're so casual, so . . . well . . . rootless. For one thing, we don't really know who you are, or where you come from, or where your family is, or even if there is a family. Perhaps for Irma's sake, I should be the one to ask you these questions."

"No," Mike said with a firm shake of his head. "No. You see, Paulette, I've made myself a rule. The girl I marry takes me on faith. If she loves me enough, it won't matter who I am, or where I've been, or where I'm going. Don't you see?"

"Why, Mike, you're an idealist!"

"Is that what you call it?" Mike grinned. "Anyway, that's the way it is."

"I see," Paulette murmured.

It was a nice approach to love, but not very practical. It might work and it might not, depending on the two people involved.

"I think you'd better get back now and rescue Irma from George Hinkle."

"George Hinkle!" Mike sighed. "You know what? There are too many George Hinkles in this world."

Laughing, they started back to the bright lights and the music. A shadow moved toward them. Instantly, Paulette recognized Ross Lane.

They met at the edge of the pool, the three of them. Ross' tie was askew, his coat was slung over his shoulder, and there was dust on his shoes. He had been walking in the desert.

"You went to see the Indian family!" Paulette said with surprise.

"I did."

"Did you tell them Johnny's going to be okay?" Mike asked.

"I said there was a chance," Ross said. "That's the truth. I still don't understand why they gave him up so easily."

"His mother could see how sick Johnny was," Paulette explained. "She knew we would help him—"

"You were strangers," Ross said harshly. "Complete strangers. Indians aren't exactly a trustful sort."

"Well, I guess it was me," Mike said easily. "I said I'd foot the bill. Money talks, you know."

"Did you know those people?" Ross asked.

Mike shrugged. "Me? Not a chance. I guess I just have an honest face. Well, I've got to go and rescue Irma. See you around."

With a wave of his hand, Mike disappeared. Ross stared after him.

"Something doesn't add up about that guy," he said.

Paulette nodded. "I know. And it worries me. Irma—"

"More than a vacation romance?" Ross asked.

"Perhaps."

She wished she hadn't run into Ross again, so soon after that scene in her room. She could feel his dark eyes probing, searching her face.

"I'll buy you a drink in the cocktail lounge," he said.

"I don't drink."

"Well, then iced coffee or something—"

"All right."

She hadn't intended to say yes. She had meant to turn him down flat, to discourage the kind of emotion she wanted to avoid, the kind they had shared only an hour or so ago.

He found a quiet table in a corner in the semi-darkened room. The coffee was iced and she sipped it leisurely. Ross leaned back to look at her.

"When are you going to tell me about him?" he asked.

She knew he meant Jim Owens.

"There's nothing to tell, Ross. It's over."

"Over for him, but not for you?" he wondered.

"Ross—"

His hand reached out and touched hers. "Look, I know I shouldn't have come to your room tonight. I was tired, dog tired. I'm still tired. When I'm like that . . . well, I let down. I thought I needed you. God knows, I wanted you—"

She shivered. His voice ran up and down her nerves like a finely pitched violin hitting a high note.

"Ross, I'm not interested in a ten-day romance. I'm not the sort. If you're trying to promote—"

He threw his head back and laughed. It took her so much by surprise that she nearly upset her coffee.

"My dear, sweet young lady! I never in my life indulged in such a thing and I've been here nearly six months. I've had my opportunities too. But believe me—there has been nothing like that."

She believed him.

"What about Judith Arnold?" she asked.

He took his hand away as if she had just burned him. A mixture of emotion was on his face again.

"You see, I know about Judith," Paulette continued. "I had supper with George Hinkle. Oh, it was quite by accident, and I couldn't avoid it. He told me you were serious about her, that you were to go into practice with her father—"

"George Hinkle!" Ross said with knotted fists. "I'd like to punch him right in his big nosey nose!"

"Then it's true?"

"Yes," Ross nodded. "It's all true. But I wasn't certain I wanted that, Paulette. I'm still not certain."

"But why here? At the Desert Plaza? Ross, I know you're a good doctor. It didn't take me long to realize that. It's such a waste—"

Ross pushed his coffee cup aside and stood up. He stretched a hand to her.

"Let's get out of here."

They left the room and she saw that he meant to take her out to his car.

"Let's drive to Sweet Springs," he said. "I'm worried about Mrs. Adams."

"You're changing the subject, Doctor."

"I know. I've already said more than I wanted to. I'm a man who likes to be certain before he says anything."

Paulette enjoyed the ride. She too was curious to know how Mrs. Adams was coming along. Ross had filled her in and it didn't sound good. At the hospital, they found her son standing by, pale and drawn.

Paulette waited outside the room while Ross went in with one of the floor nurses. When he came out, Paulette's heart leaped. There was a grin on his face.

"She's better, Paulette. Stronger in every way. Matter of fact, she wants to see you."

Paulette nodded and went in. She knew better than to stay long, and her training had taught her the right things to say. The old woman smiled and gripped her hand. Her son gave her an appreciative grin as she said goodbye and left.

Ross made a few notes on her chart, looked in on Johnny

and then they left the hospital again. But Ross didn't go directly back to the hotel. Instead, he headed down the highway in the opposite direction. The road was straight and white in the starlight, and traffic was not heavy. Ross drove faster and faster. It was an exhilarating ride. Ross had firm control of the wheel and she understood his need for speed, he used it to chase away problems, ease his tensions.

Finally, he slowed the car, turned around, and they started back.

"I haven't done that in a long time," he confessed. "As a boy, I used to run. I'd run as fast as I could for as long as I could, until I ached all over for want of air. But it was a good feeling. A cleansing thing."

"I understand."

"Only I never could last as long as Dave."

"Dave?"

"My friend. We were good friends."

"Is he a doctor too?"

She saw how his hands tightened on the wheel. He shook his head.

"Dave's dead. He died when he was sixteen."

"I'm sorry."

They said no more. She understood that Dave, whoever he had been, had been very important to Ross. Somehow, Dave was all mixed up in this night and the way Ross was behaving.

The lights of the hotel loomed ahead. The dance was still going on, but it was getting late.

Couples were beginning to leave the dance and return to their rooms. In the lobby, they spied George Hinkle being super-attentive to a stylish woman several years older than he. Ross looked at Paulette and they both laughed. At least Irma had escaped his clutches.

Ross saw Paulette to her door. He unlocked it for her, but kept her from going inside.

"Wait a minute. Tomorrow afternoon, I should be free. I'd like to drive up into the mountains to Rugged Rock—my old home town. I don't want to go alone. Would you come with me?"

"Are you sure you want me along?"

Ross nodded. His dark eyes burned and lingered for a moment on her face. "Yes, I'm sure."

"All right."

He bent his head to kiss her. She had anticipated it and yet did nothing to stop him. Almost willingly, she went into his arms. For one moment at least, she forgot Jim Owens. Later, she wondered if he had forgotten Judith Arnold.

XII

IRMA WAS a lumpy heap in her twin bed, hair mussed, pug nose burrowed into a pillow. She and Mike had made quite a night of it. Paulette had been in bed an hour or two before she heard Irma come in.

It was late. Paulette had lain quietly, not wanting to disturb Irma, but now it was simply time to be up and stirring. Paulette opened the draperies to the bright, sunlit day. Her eyes strayed for a moment toward the mountains and she wondered what Rugged Rock was going to be like. She wondered too why Ross had asked her to go with him. Somehow she sensed it was to be a sentimental sort of journey. Most men would have preferred to go alone.

"Oooh, what is that light?" Irma murmured behind her.

Paulette laughed and went to shake her friend.

"Come on, sleepyhead. It's nearly ten o'clock. And I have a date this afternoon."

"Oh, leave me in peace!" Irma wailed.

"Not a chance," Paulette said.

Paulette grabbed a pillow and began to thump Irma with it. Irma thumped back. They began to laugh, swatting each other, tumbling over the bed and causing an uproar. If they weren't careful the manager would be pounding on the door and demanding silence. But it wasn't the manager that interrupted them. It was the phone.

"Hello," Paulette answered, a little breathless.

"Paulette, the doctor was supposed to be here by ten and he hasn't shown up. Listen, I'm going to get out of this bed. Whether anyone is here or not—"

"Hold on, Boyd. Calm down. I'll be right there."

Irma made a face as Paulette hung up.

"He's using you, kiddo," Irma said. "He calls and you jump. How come?"

Paulette shrugged. "I don't know. I guess it's habit. When someone yells for help, I go running."

"Well, this isn't Bryson General!" Irma protested. "It's the Desert Plaza and honestly, all you've done since you got here is look after people—"

Paulette gave her red hair a couple of strokes with the hairbrush and checked her lipstick.

"I've been happy. Really, Irma. Don't worry about it. You and Mike must have had some evening last night."

"I could have killed him!" Irma burst out. "He let George Hinkle lead me around that dance floor for an hour before he finally cut in!"

"That's a man for you," Paulette laughed. "Go ahead and eat your breakfast. Mike's probably waiting for you. I'll see you later."

Irma was still calling her protests as Paulette left the room and closed the door behind her. She could have ignored Boyd, she supposed. But on the other hand, he was just foolish and stubborn enough to get out of bed without help.

Paulette took the stairs up to the fifth floor. The climb nearly winded her.

She tapped lightly at Boyd's door.

"Come in, come in!" he called.

Boyd grinned when he saw her. She was aware of how devilishly handsome this man was. He was sitting up in bed. His eyes were clear and his color was good. From all indications Boyd Sheridan was making a very rapid recovery.

"If you'll hand me my robe, I'll put it on and maybe we can go out on the balcony."

"Boyd, are you certain—"

"Look, I'm getting up!" Boyd said angrily. "Do I make myself clear?"

"Gracious, you must be feeling better. You're getting cranky. That's always a sure sign."

She helped him on with his robe. Rather gingerly, he put his feet on the floor and stood up. Paulette watched him closely. With a grin, he draped an arm around her shoulder and leaned on her.

"Hey, look! I'm on my feet and I'm not even thinking about passing out."

He leaned on her all the way. On the balcony, she helped him into a chair. He sat there, breathing deeply of the fresh air. Then he reached for her hand and held it for a moment.

"You're a good little nurse, Paulette."

"Thank you."

He raised her fingers to his lips and kissed them. She tried to pull away, but couldn't; his grip was strong and persistent.

"I don't know what's been the matter with me," he confessed. "You're just what I like in a woman and I've sure made plenty of stupid mistakes—"

"Boyd—"

The phone rang inside. He frowned and checked his wristwatch. "Surely can't be the old man this time of day. He never sees bed before two or three."

"I'll answer it for you," Paulette said. "Maybe it's Doctor Lane."

Boyd protested, but she stepped inside and picked up the phone.

"Hello," she said.

"Who in thunder is this?" a voice bellowed.

"Paulette Castle. Would you like to speak to Boyd?"

"What are you doing in Boyd's room?"

"Looking after him," Paulette replied, her cheeks burning pink. "Who is this, please."

"This happens to be Sheridan! Who else? And what do you mean, looking after him?"

"Boyd had a slight accident. I'm a registered nurse, Mr. Sheridan."

"Nurse! What is this? Now listen here, young lady—"

Boyd was beckoning wildly from the balcony but Paulette ignored him. She let the older man rave and rant on the other end of the line. When he finally had run down, she explained again in no uncertain terms. It took him by surprise, for there was a long silence on the other end of the line.

"Boyd was thrown, was he? Darned fool. Riding is for kids. I've told him to stay off horses. Put him on the line, young lady."

She carried the phone out to the balcony and Boyd took the receiver with a wry face. Paulette saw how he stiffened, as if preparing himself for battle.

"Boyd!"

The older Sheridan was bellowing so loudly, that Paulette could hear both ends of the conversation.

"I'm right here. I haven't got the report ready, if that's what you want. As Miss Castle told you, I haven't been quite myself—"

There was a string of hot, angry words and Boyd held the receiver away from his ear.

"I'll get it as soon as I possibly can!" Boyd managed to say.

"You do that, boy. You got another twenty-four hours. Cracked head or no cracked head."

The older Sheridan hung up with a bang. Boyd handed the receiver back to Paulette. He looked pale and tired. The call had upset him. She saw him reach into his robe pocket for a couple of mints and pop them into his mouth. He gnashed them angrily between his teeth.

"Surely your father doesn't expect you to conduct business when you're ill!" Paulette exclaimed.

"You don't know my father," Boyd replied. "He's as hard as nails. He gets what he wants. He wants this hotel if it's worth the investment."

"The Desert Plaza!"

"That's right. I'm here to evaluate it. I'm trusting you to keep this confidential."

"Of course. So that's the business you're in."

Boyd shrugged. "I go out and do the leg work. I don't dare make a mistake either. I bought a big flop once and I haven't heard the end of it yet."

She felt sorry for Boyd. He seemed so upset. His father's call had undone him.

"Why do you take it, Boyd?" she asked.

"I don't know," he said miserably. "I really don't know."

"A sense of loyalty?"

"I suppose," Boyd sighed. "I've thought of quitting plenty of times. If he rides me about this deal while I'm still half out on my feet—"

Paulette touched his shoulder lightly with her hand. He jumped. His nerves were wound as tight as piano wires.

"Have you had breakfast, Boyd? Could I order something for you?"

"Would you eat with me?" he asked.

"All right."

She called room service. While they waited for breakfast to arrive, they sat quietly on the balcony. Boyd had his head back, eyes closed. She wondered what was going through his mind.

Their food came. The boy set up a small table for them on the balcony and served them. Boyd tipped him, then waved him away.

"When I eat breakfast with a beautiful girl, I sure don't need anyone hovering over my shoulder."

The boy left with a grin. Paulette poured their coffee while Boyd watched her closely, his gray eyes blazing.

"How would you always like to pour my coffee?"

He leaned over then and kissed her. It was not the sort of kiss she would have expected from him. It was rather boyish and awkward. It touched her. He was about to kiss her again when they became aware of someone standing in the door.

Paulette's heart jumped. Ross Lane thumped his bag into an empty chair.

"Well, seems you're feeling much better, Boyd."

Boyd smiled. "I do. Paulette helped me out here. I feel fit as a fiddle."

Ross was angry. There were little white lines around his mouth. Paulette stared down at her hands, wondering how it was that she could be trapped into so many embarrassing situations.

Ross took Boyd's pulse and checked the bruise on his head.

"Any nausea?" he asked.

"No."

"Weakness in your arms or legs?"

Boyd shook his head.

"Any dizziness? Sight okay?"

"I'm fine, Doc," Boyd said. Then, with a direct glance at Paulette, he added, "In fact, I never felt better. I can't remember when I've enjoyed a breakfast so much."

Ross didn't miss the implication. His jaw tightened. He bent to pick up his bag. "It seems you're going to recover. Stay up for an hour or so. Then rest an hour. Do that alternately until you're sure you feel like your old self."

As he started to go, Paulette called him back. "Ross, have you been to the hospital this morning?"

"Yes," Ross nodded.

"Mrs. Adams?"

"A good night. She's going to be all right."

"And Johnny?"

Ross hesitated, for only a moment, but Paulette sensed the flicker of worry in his face. "About the same. He's still a very sick boy. He has a weak heart on top of everything else. Now if you'll excuse me, I have people waiting in my office."

He let himself out. The minute the door was closed, Boyd laughed.

"Get him! He was about fit to be tied when he saw you here. Has he staked a claim on you too, Paulette?"

"No one has staked a claim on me!" she replied hotly. "I am not a piece of merchandise that you buy! Like a hotel!"

"Whee," Boyd grinned. "There's some real temper under that red hair, isn't there? Hey, where are you going?"

She was moving rapidly toward the door. Boyd was out of his chair and chasing after her. He caught her before she could escape him.

"Whoa there," he said thoughtfully. "I didn't mean to sound . . . well . . . you know what I mean."

"No, I'm afraid I don't, Boyd. I never knew anyone like you before!"

His shoulders sagged. "You're right. I'm getting more like my old man every day. I'm sorry, Paulette. I really am. Don't go away mad."

He pulled her close for a moment. She tried to resist but he was strong.

"You should be in bed!" she said crossly.

He pushed her back so he could see her face and grinned. "I'll go to bed soon. I promise. I'll do just what the doctor says if you'll say you're not mad at me."

"Oh, Boyd!"

"Say it," he said, shaking her gently.

"All right. It's forgotten."

He kissed her again. It would have done no good to try and stop him. Again the sincerity of the kiss stunned her.

"I may be calculating like my old man and a little boorish sometimes too, but I know what I want when I see it. And I want you, Paulette Castle. I think I'm falling in love with you. Get that. Me, Boyd Sheridan!"

"That blow on your head was worse than we thought," she said quickly. "Get back to bed, lover boy."

Then she wiggled out of his arm and escaped him. She took a moment to compose herself. She wondered if Ross still wanted her to go with him now. How on earth could a vacation get so complicated?

Her phone was ringing when she reached her room. Irma

had gone. Snatching it up, she was surprised to hear Ross' voice.

"Would one o'clock be all right with you?" he asked.

"Yes. That would be fine."

"See you then."

He hung up. Paulette sank to the bed as she replaced the receiver. So it was still on. But why should Ross be angry? He had no claim on her. No one had a claim on her.

She thought of Jim Owens. He no longer had a claim either. When had that happened? What had finally knocked him out of her system? Was it Ross Lane or Boyd Sheridan? The awful part of it was, she didn't know. Both men were attractive. Both had something to offer. Both were interesting—widely different, but interesting.

Here she was, trying to guard Irma from getting hurt and from getting in too deep, and she had forgotten to watch herself. The vacation was going so swiftly. Just another few days left. It might be two very sadly disillusioned girls who got on the train to Bryson.

Paulette shivered at the thought of Bryson, dreading to go back there. Her hospital job was satisfactory, even satisfying in a mild sort of way. But she wanted more. And she didn't know what it was she wanted or needed. Everything was getting more confused with each day, more complicated.

But at least there was this afternoon's drive with Ross to think about. When she got back, she knew Boyd would be waiting. It was a merry-go-round and she had no idea where or when it was going to stop.

XIII

Ross was prompt, knocking on Paulette's door at one o'clock sharp. She was ready and a little nervous about the whole thing. Irma, when she heard about it, had been all for it.

"Look, you need to have some fun. The drive up into the mountains will be nice."

But then Irma didn't know what Paulette did. Most of all, she hoped there wouldn't be any discussion about Boyd Sheridan between them. She wished she had a few more minutes in which to compose herself, but here was Ross at the door.

"Ready?" he asked, his dark eyes taking her in with one glance.

"Ready," she murmured. "It's a lovely day for the drive, isn't it?"

"I hope you aren't expecting too much," he answered. "Rugged Rock isn't much of a town."

His voice sounded hesitant, uncertain. Even now, as they left the hotel, he wasn't sure he really wanted to go back there.

He saw her into the car, and soon they were leaving the hotel behind. He took a road she had seen from the trail ride, nosing directly toward the mountains.

"How long has it been since you've been back?" she asked.

"Several years."

"No family?"

"A cousin or two. I've lost touch. My parents are dead. My mother died when I was a boy. I think that's when I began to hang around with Dave so much."

Dave again. A good friend who had died at the age of sixteen. There were little hard gleams of light in Ross' eyes. His grip was tight and tense on the steering wheel.

"Are you certain you want to go?" Paulette asked gently. "If you want to change your mind—"

He shook his head quickly. "No, I must go, Paulette. I've been sitting in the Desert Plaza trying to get up nerve enough to come for six months. Now—I'm going."

He didn't seem to want to talk any more, so Paulette fastened her eyes to the passing landscape. In just a few minutes they were into the foothills. The road was narrow and not too smooth. Now and then she glanced down into a deep canyon and it nearly took her breath away. But Ross, even though he had not been here for several years, seemed to remember the road.

The cool air was refreshing. The mountains were rugged, sharply jutted, and majestic in their own right.

"We're nearly there," Ross said. "Another mile or so. In the next valley."

She was filled with anticipation, uncertain what to expect. Suddenly the road turned downward in hairpin curves and then abruptly, like an island appearing in a vast sea, there was the town of Rugged Rock.

It was an odd mixture. Most of it was shabby, the buildings incredibly old and needing paint. The streets were narrow.

"They used to do a lot of mining here," Ross told her. "There's still a little. It's all that keeps the town going— That and the tourists who come through."

There wasn't a modern building in the place except one new gas station. The place reeked of years, of hard times, and of people who perhaps had begun simply not to care.

Ross braked to a stop. He was still gripping the wheel tightly, his dark eyes looking around with a hungry expression. Paulette touched his arm and he jumped.

"Where did you live?" she asked.

"I'll show you. Let's walk. There's never any room to park a car along these streets."

The sun bore down on them. Curious eyes turned in their direction. Paulette expected someone to remember Ross and call to him, but no one did. A small group of ragged Indian

103

children stared at them. Ross thrust his hand deep into his pocket and found some coins. He tossed them into the air and the children scrambled for them with squeals of delight, fighting over them.

"The poor little devils," Ross breathed.

An old Indian Squaw, perched alongside the street, waved some Indian woven baskets at them, asking them to buy. But Ross ignored her and tugged Paulette into a faster walk.

"They think we're tourists," Ross said.

When they reached the place where the house should have been, they found only a rubbish-filled vacant lot. Ross stared in disbelief. Obviously a fire had destroyed it, for a few charred rafters still reached skyward.

"Well, so much for that," he said. "Maybe it's just as well. It wasn't much better than the other houses around here, Paulette. As you can see, my beginnings were of the humble sort."

"And what about Dave?"

"Dave lived just a couple of blocks away. I don't want to go there."

"Where are Dave's people?"

"Scattered so far as I know."

They continued to walk. Paulette saw the store where Ross and Dave had bought candy, the junk yard that had purchased old bottles and scrap iron from them, the mining office where Ross' father had once worked, and the school Ross had attended.

"Isn't there a doctor here?" Paulette asked.

Ross shook his head. "No. The nearest one is at Sweet Springs."

"But Sweet Springs is several miles away!" Paulette said. "What do they do in case of emergency?"

Ross set his jaw in a hard way. "They do the best they can—just as they always have. The Indians treat themselves. The whites—most of them—can get to Sweet Springs. But not all."

"I see."

"There used to be one decent place to eat in town. Let's have some coffee."

The café was hopelessly shabby, like the rest of the town. Surely Rugged Rock was dying. In time, Paulette was certain it would be as desolate as Gold Corners.

The coffee was hot and strong. Ross stirred his, deep in thought. He looked suddenly very tired.

"We used to come here, Dave and I, whenever we had any spending money. It wasn't often we could afford it. We'd eat bowls of chili and stale crackers. Or maybe, if we were real flush, we'd have a steak sandwich."

Paulette reached across the scarred table and took his long fingers in her hand. "Ross, you mustn't grieve so, after all these years. It's wrong—"

Ross' eyes brightened for a moment with unashamed tears.

"I know. But he's all around me here. He was the only brother I had, Paulette—the only real friend. Then I lost him because his parents were stupid! Yes, that's what I said—stupid! Ignorant. They let him die without a doctor."

Paulette felt a tingle of shock. "Without a doctor?"

"That's hard to believe, isn't it? We're used to all the modern drugs, the newest techniques, the best equipped hospitals, the sterile facilities! But just a few years ago Dave died of pneumonia in a stinking, dirty, windy tent!"

Paulette saw the raw hurt in Ross' eyes. He was gripping her hand so hard it hurt, but she didn't cry out. Tent!

"Ross, was Dave an—"

"Indian," Ross said quietly. "A fullblooded Navajo Indian."

Now things began to fall into place.

"So that's why you defended them so hotly the other day," she murmured. "But then why were you so reluctant to care for Johnny?"

"I wasn't reluctant. It wasn't that at all. Maybe I was afraid to get involved with the Indians again. Ever since I've been at the Desert Plaza, I haven't let myself come home here to Rugged Rock. Everything tells me it's foolish to even consider coming back."

"Coming back!" she exclaimed. "You mean you want to practice here?"

Ross closed his eyes tiredly. "I don't know. I'd be a fool, wouldn't I? What's here? Nothing! I'd work like a crazy man and not be paid. There's no one here to help me. Half the town is Indian. Woud they trust me? Would they let me help them—"

"And you took the job at the Desert Plaza to have time to think about it," she said. "I understand now."

"Judith is against the idea, of course. I was foolish enough to think that if a woman loved a man, it wouldn't matter what he did for a living, or where he practiced his craft. It seems I was mistaken. Judith wants the gay social life of New York. She wants a society doctor for a husband."

"I see." Paulette nodded. "But what do *you* want to do? Deep down in your own heart?"

Ross shook his head. "I still don't know. Maybe it's that I do know and I'm afraid to admit it to myself. I think I want to come back. But it would be a hard battle. I'm not certain I'm up to it, Paulette. I'm not certain I can do this alone."

"Do you love Judith Arnold?" Paulette asked in a low voice. "That's the real deciding factor, isn't it?"

Ross pushed aside his coffee, half drunk, and met her eyes.

"She's very attractive. She has a magnetic personality. I'm afraid she can twist me around her little finger."

"But do you love her?" Paulette persisted.

Ross got to his feet. "Let's go, Paulette."

They went back to the car. Before driving back to the hotel, he went through the other end of town. Here, in the Indian section of town, conditions were even worse. Paulette's heart twisted. Just as she had wanted to help Johnny when she had found him so ill in the ragged tent out in the foothills, she wished she could help these people too.

"It tears your heart out," she sighed. "Oh, Ross, if only we could—"

"Yes? Go on."

"Nothing," she shook her head. "It was only a wild, crazy thought."

She had been about to say, if only we could come here, the two of us as a team, and help them—care for them, teach them the fundamentals of good health. But they weren't a team. In a few days she would be returning to Bryson and perhaps Ross would be going back to Judith Arnold.

Ross stopped the car again. There was a small burial ground here. Cairns marked the graves.

"I'd like to go alone, Paulette."

"Of course."

She watched Ross walk away, head down, shoulders set against the emotions that rocked him. For a long time, he stood beside one of the cairns, the wind stirring his dark hair. When he came back, his eyes were red rimmed and his shoulders were sagging. They said nothing as he started the car and turned it around.

They sped quickly through Rugged Rock and up into the winding hairpin curves. He didn't speak again until they had reached the open highway, with the mountains behind them.

"Thanks for coming, Paulette. It was much easier than coming alone."

"I'll never forget this drive, Ross. Not as long as I live."

"I'll drop you at the hotel. Then I'd better check my patients at the hospital. I'm anxious to know if Johnny has responded to the medication yet."

"Let me know when you get back, will you, Ross?"

"Sure thing."

He dropped her at the main entrance of the Desert Plaza, waved, and drove away. How abruptly the world had changed. It was hard to imagine that a few miles away a town like Rugged Rock existed, almost within the shadow of the luxurious Desert Plaza. Most of the people that came here scarcely knew about Rugged Rock, and most certainly didn't care. They had come for a vacation, and a chance to forget their own cares. But Paulette wondered if she would ever be able to forget the faces of those Indians she had seen. They would haunt her the rest of her life.

Paulette walked briskly across the lobby. A voice called to her. It was Mike Allan.

"We've been watching for you. Come join us for awhile."

Irma was stretched out lazily in a lounge chair near the pool, looking sunburned, relaxed, and happy. Mike pulled over a chair for Paulette. A few swimmers were still splashing about in the water. From the tennis court someone was shouting encouragement. There was the tinkle of ice in glasses, the smell of sun lotion, the padding of bare feet across the hot patio.

"You're awfully quiet," Irma pointed out. "Wasn't the drive fun?"

"No," Paulette frowned. "Fun wasn't the word for it. Revealing is better."

"Want to talk about it?" Mike asked.

"Not right now. Tell me, what have you been doing all afternoon?"

"Nothing," Mike said. "Just nothing. We've been lazy. Talked. Laughed. We thought about driving into Sweet Springs, but we were just too tired."

"Paulette, do you know how many days we have left?" Irma asked.

"Five," she replied.

"Time's going so fast," Irma wailed.

"Let's not waste a minute of it," Mike said cheerfully. "Let's plan something wild and terrific for tonight. You join us, Paulette."

"No, I think not. I want to wait for Ross to come back from the hospital. I'm anxious about Johnny."

"There you go again, worrying about people," Irma grinned.

"At least have dinner with us," Mike said.

"All right. Now I think I'll go up to my room and leave you two lazy people to your own devices."

Later, dressing for dinner, Paulette tried twice to phone Ross, but apparently he hadn't returned. He was staying a very long time at the hospital.

Going downstairs with Irma to the dining room where Mike

waited for them, Paulette was startled to find Boyd Sheridan in the elevator.

"Well, hello!" he said, pleased. "You're back! And I'm certainly glad of that. Now I won't have to eat alone."

"You shouldn't be here!" Paulette protested. "You were to stay in your room."

Boyd shook his head. "I'm fine, I tell you. I've been up all afternoon. I'm fit as a fiddle. Come on, beautiful, stop being a nurse for five minutes, will you?"

Paulette had to laugh. "All right. You win. But I won't be responsible if you have a relapse."

"Fair enough."

He offered her his arm as they left the elevator. Mike saw them and grinned.

"Good, we'll make it a foursome. How you feeling, Boyd?"

"I don't want to be asked that again tonight. Do I make myself clear?" Boyd asked with a smile.

"Okay, okay," Mike grinned. "Let's put on the feedbag."

It was a pleasant group. Mike kept them laughing. Boyd had set himself to charm Paulette and his attentions were flattering. Irma could hardly take her eyes off Mike and Paulette still had misgivings about that. It was getting serious, much too serious. There were still too many question marks about Mike in Paulette's mind.

They had reached the dessert course when Paulette looked up and saw Ross in the doorway. She knew instantly that there was something very much wrong. He caught her eye. Then, seeing Boyd with her, he turned to go.

"Excuse me," Paulette said quickly, dropping her napkin to the table.

She hurried out of the dining room and caught Ross at the elevator.

"What is it?" she asked. "Ross—"

"Johnny," he murmured. "Johnny didn't make it. He died an hour ago."

He turned to her with a face that was tired and drained of emotion.

XIV

"OH, NO!" Paulette gasped. "I had no idea that tick fever could be fatal!"

"It isn't generally," Ross said in a weary voice. "But Johnny was run down, and I told you his heart wasn't good either. Probably a condition he'd had since birth. He simply wasn't strong enough to fight off the infection—"

By now, Boyd, Mike, and Irma had joined them, and they had heard the news. Irma's eyes brightened with tears and Mike knotted his fists.

"The poor kid," Mike murmured. "The poor little kid!"

"What about the family? Do they know?" Paulette asked.

"The mother was there," Ross said. "She'd walked to the hospital. I brought her home. The father and the sister—well, I suppose they're finding out about it now."

"I'd like to speak with them," Paulette said.

"I'm not sure that's a good idea," Ross frowned. "They're bound to be upset."

"I want them to know I care," Paulette said fiercely. "Please, Ross—"

"I can't stop you," he replied. "Go if you want. I'll talk to them myself a little later. I have some important calls to make."

"I'll go with you," Mike spoke up. "They trusted me. Come along, Paulette."

"I'll wait here for you," Irma said.

"Must you do this?" Boyd protested with a frown.

Paulette gave him a quick look. "I must."

Boyd shrugged. "Okay. I'll wait with Irma."

Mike took Paulette's arm and they walked out of the hotel. It was getting dark now. They could still see the pathetic tent pitched some distance away.

"Mike, what will we say to them? What can we say? They trusted us to make Johnny well and now—he's dead!"

"That's why I came along," Mike said thoughtfully. "There might be trouble. Right now we have no idea what they're thinking."

"You know them well, Mike?"

Mike shrugged. "Well enough."

They walked swiftly, both eager to have this over and done with. The Indian family heard them and saw them coming. They were a tight little knot of three mourners around a tiny fire where supper had been started and now abandoned. The mother was moaning, rocking back and forth, holding her arms closely around her body.

The father stepped out and glared at them. Mike offered his hand.

"Sorry, sir. We did all we could, but your boy had a bad heart. Something he was born with. Sorry."

Paulette, too, extended her hand, and for a moment the father took it. Then Paulette embraced the little girl and the mother, in a way that spoke more eloquently than words.

Mike was taking his wallet out of his pocket. He pressed a number of bills into the Indian's hand.

"You're a good man, Mike Allan," the Indian said.

"Don't worry about the bills. Use this as you see fit. If there's anything you want, you come to the hotel and get me."

The Indian nodded, gripping the bills tightly in his dark fist.

Mike took Paulette's arm. "Come, I think it's time to go."

"I want the doctor," the Indian said with steel in his voice. "I want that doctor—"

"He'll be out to see you," Paulette said. "Very soon now."

The Indian nodded. "I'll wait."

Mike tugged her away. She cast one sympathetic glance over her shoulder at the mourning family.

"I didn't like the way he said that," Mike murmured. "About the doctor, I mean. It might be a good idea if Ross stayed away for awhile."

"What do you mean, Mike?"

"They blame Ross for losing their son," Mike said.

"They can't!" Paulette exclaimed. "It makes no sense."

"Only one thing makes sense to them," Mike explained— "the fact that Johnny is dead and that Ross was the doctor."

They tramped away from the tent, toward the hotel. Paulette felt a ripple of fear for Ross. Surely Mike was mistaken.

"Mike, did that family know you?"

Mike shook his head. "Not really. Perhaps they had heard of me."

"They trusted you immediately. Wasn't that a little odd?"

"Don't worry about it," Mike said.

They had reached the hotel. The lights were bright and rather mocking.

"I'll go talk to Ross," Mike said. "Join the others."

She wasn't certain she wanted to join them, but she did. Irma was asking questions as fast as she could and Boyd stood back, studying her with interested eyes.

Mike returned.

"I didn't see Ross," he said. "He's busy with a patient somewhere in the hotel. I left a message for him to look me up."

The dance was starting. Boyd nodded toward the floor.

"Come on, beautiful; let's give it a whirl."

Paulette shook her head. "I'm sorry, Boyd. I just don't feel like dancing right now. And for that matter, I think you've been up long enough. You ought to go to your room and rest."

Boyd laughed and took her arm. "Then we'll have a little stroll. I want to talk to you."

Boyd led her away from Mike and Irma. Outside, the clean desert air smelled good. They found a quiet, unoccupied spot hidden in the shadows. There, Boyd took Paulette into his arms and kissed her soundly.

"I love you, Paulette Castle."

Despite her determination to resist this man, her heart jumped. It wasn't every day someone told her that he loved her.

"Boyd—"

"No. Let me talk. I've fallen in love with you, Paulette. I want to marry you."

She was too stunned to say anything. But she was almost glad that a bellboy began to page Boyd just then. With a mutter of annoyance, he made his presence known.

"Yes, what is it?" Boyd asked.

"Telephone, sir," the boy told him.

Boyd hesitated. "I suppose it's the old man again!"

"You'd better go."

"Don't move. I'll be right back."

Boyd's footsteps rang out harshly over the patio flagstone. Paulette's eyes strayed outward toward the Indian tent. Her heart bled for those poor people. The mother's moaning in grief would linger inside her for a long while.

Boyd was gone only a few minutes. When he came back, his hand was dipping into his coat pocket and he was popping mints into his mouth.

"What happened?" she asked.

"I got my orders to move on," he said. "He's decided against buying the Desert Plaza."

"I see. Are you up to traveling?"

"I'd better be," Boyd laughed curtly. "You don't cross the Old Man."

He popped three more mints into his mouth and she could hear him crunch them angrily with his teeth.

"Why go?" she asked quietly. "Why jump when he cracks the whip?"

"I don't know," Boyd confessed. "Maybe I'm spineless."

"You keep on like this, Boyd, and you're going to crack one of these days."

He took her by the shoulders, resting his hands there lightly.

"Stop being a nurse, will you? Be a woman, at least on my last night here."

He kissed her then—the same sincere, warm sort of kiss he had given her before.

"Come with me," he said. "Come with me, Paulette."

"So I can jump, too, whenever your father tells me to? I wouldn't like that. I would get to hate it—and you."

"You don't mean that," Boyd said. "You find me attractive, don't you? We'd make a great pair! Think of all the traveling we could do, the things we could see. And my father gives me a nice expense account. I'll show you how to live, Paulette."

"My values are different than yours, Boyd. I wouldn't be happy that way. I'd feel so useless—"

"Useless!" he exclaimed. "Not when you were making me a happy man! That wouldn't be useless."

"Tell me, would you part ways with your father for me?"

Boyd tightened his arms around her. "What's that got to do with it?"

"Would you?"

"It's my job. I'm trained in the work—"

She pulled out of his arms. "I would never be happy in that sort of set-up. In your own way, you're dedicated, Boyd. You'll never leave your father. In fact, I don't think you hate it as much as you pretend. Besides, I'm a nurse. I'll always be a nurse. I want to help people—"

"Paulette! Paulette!"

It was Mike calling her. He sounded excited. He came bursting out of the shadows toward them.

"Here, Mike. What is it?" she asked.

"That darned fool went out there. He didn't see me before he left."

"You mean Ross?" Paulette asked with alarm.

"That's exactly who I mean. He's gone out there alone. I'm going after him."

"I'll go with you."

"No," Boyd said angrily. "You're staying here with me. I'm not through talking to you yet. For crying out loud, Paulette—"

She reached up and patted his cheek. In a way, she felt

sorry for him. For awhile she had even been attracted to him, but now it was all over.

"Don't wait for me, Boyd. It would never work out."

Then, with Mike tugging at her hand, she said goodbye and hurried away.

"We'll take my car," Mike said. "It's used to rough driving."

The car was impossibly old. Paulette was surprised that it started, but it did. With a roar, they were off, heading straight for the tent. There was no road, just the open desert. Paulette feared they would mire down in the sand, but Mike pushed on, the headlights piercing the darkness.

"What's that?" Paulette asked. "Mike, stop the car!"

The figure lay crumpled in the sand, a white shirt showing in the dark.

"My God, it's Ross!" Paulette screamed. "Mike—help me, help me!"

She knelt beside him. With quick fingers she examined him. Mike came running with a flashlight. Ross' shirt was stained with blood. Paulette ripped it away.

"A stab wound!" Mike said. "That Indian—that stupid Indian—"

"Help me get him into the car. We've got to get him to the hospital. Mike, do you have a first aid kit in the car?"

"Sure. I'll get it."

There was little she could do, but she pressed a bandage against the bleeding wound in Ross' side. It was impossible to tell how deep or how severe the stab wound was, but she prayed it was only superficial.

Ross stirred as they worked over him.

"Lie still, Ross," Paulette told him. "It's okay. We're here. We'll take care of you."

"There was a fight," he moaned. "He came at me with a knife."

"I'll kill him for this!" Mike muttered.

"No," Ross said, licking his dry lips. "It wasn't his fault. He was half crazy with grief and he'd got hold of some whiskey somewhere. He was whiskey crazy—"

"My fault," Mike said grimly. "I shouldn't have given him the money. I know better. Mike Allan, number one idiot."

"Help me lift him," Paulette said. "Easy now."

They got Ross to his feet and he fainted. It took all of their strength to get him into Mike's old car. Then, with a roar, they were off again. Mike drove the old car with the gas pedal to the floor, muttering to himself all the way.

To Paulette, there had never been such a long ride. Would the lights of Sweet Springs never show in the darkness?

"Hurry, Mike!"

"I am," he said impatiently. "I should have come in the Cadillac!"

The old car was vibrating with the speed. Paulette prayed it would hold together until they reached the hospital.

"There!" Mike shouted triumphantly. "There it is!"

Thank God, Paulette thought. Thank the sweet God!

They went chugging up the emergency entrance. The car shivered to a stop. At Mike's call, attendants came running with a stretcher. Then Ross was lifted out. In the bright lights, Paulette saw that blood had seeped through the bandage she had taped to his side. He was ghostly white, his skin moist and his pulse weak. There was no luster in his eyes. Everything pointed to shock. He was going into shock!

"It's all right, miss," the attendant said. "We'll take care of him. Tell us what happened if you can."

"I'll tell you," Mike said heavily. "A half crazy Indian stabbed him. He's lost a lot of blood. We found him lying in the sand, halfway back to the hotel—"

"Take it easy, buddy," the attendant said. "Why don't you and the lady go have some coffee? We'll take care of the doctor."

They let him be wheeled away. Paulette covered her face with her hands and the sobs started. Mike patted her shoulder awkwardly.

"Take it easy, Paulette. We've done all we could. Now we'll let the hospital do the rest. Come on."

She let Mike lead her away. Mike phoned the hotel and told Irma what had happened. Then he came back and they sat in chairs in the waiting room, heads down. The hands on the clock scarcely moved.

"He's being taken to surgery now," they were told at last.

Paulette gripped her hands together, knowing what was going on. She had stood beside the operating table more than once herself. She had handed instruments to the surgeon; she had listened to the patient's condition being read out in a quiet voice, for the surgeon to hear. What were they saying about Ross? Was his heartbeat strong and steady. How was his respiration? How deeply had the knife entered? Had a vital organ been damaged?

"It's taking so long," she said.

Mike nodded. "It seems a year. You love him, don't you, Paulette? You're in love with the guy!"

Two hot tears trickled down her face. She nodded tiredly, and with almost a sense of relief she admitted the truth to herself.

"Yes. I'm in love with Ross, Mike. Really in love. In a way I never even knew of before. It's for keeps this time. This is for real."

But the hands on the clock still barely moved and upstairs, under glaring lights, Ross lay quiet and still on an operating table, put there because he tried to help the Indians. He must hate them now. He would have turned against them. What would this do to a man like Ross? She didn't even want to think about it.

They looked up at last to see a nurse coming toward them, a tired surgeon following her. Paulette got to her feet and couldn't even feel her legs or her arms or any sensation in her body as she waited for the doctor to speak.

XV

"THE SURGERY went well," the doctor said. "The wound was deep but luck was with him. There was no serious damage done."

Paulette felt her legs begin to sag. If Mike hadn't put his arm around her, she might have crumpled to the floor.

"Thank God!" she murmured.

"He's going to be okay?" Mike asked. "Really okay?"

"Yes," the surgeon nodded.

"May I see him?" Paulette asked.

"He's still drowsy, and it's getting late. Why don't you come back tomorrow, Miss Castle? He'll be ready for visitors then."

"That makes sense," Mike agreed. "Come along, Paulette. They're waiting for news at the hotel."

She wanted to see Ross, but she let herself be persuaded to leave. The first thing in the morning, she would be back.

The drive to the hotel in Mike's old car was a silent one. When they reached the gaily lighted resort, Paulette went straight to her room. Irma was there, pacing the floor.

"How is he?" she asked.

"All right. He's going to be all right," Paulette said.

"Where's Mike?"

"Downstairs. I think he was rather shaken by all this. He gave money to Johnny's father and he bought whiskey with it. Probably right here at the hotel. He attacked Ross—"

Irma shuddered. "How awful. And after all Ross tried to do for Johnny."

"Well, it's over now," Paulette sighed. "And I'm very tired."

"Let's hit the sack," Irma decided.

"Mike may want to see you."

"But I don't want to see him," Irma replied. "Not just yet. Paulette, he asked me to marry him."

Paulette raised her head to look at her friend. Irma sounded uncertain.

"What did you say?" Paulette asked.

"What could I say? I don't know. I—I love the guy, Paulette, but I always said I'd never marry a fellow like him. He's so carefree with money. He doesn't even have a steady job. Oh, Paulette, I almost wish we hadn't come here for our vacation."

"What do you want me to say?"

"Anything!" Irma pleaded. "Tell me what to do."

Paulette shook her head. "I can't do that. You have to decide yourself. But if you let him go, Irma, will you ever be happy again?"

"I doubt it!" Irma sighed. "I doubt it very much."

"Maybe that's your answer. Listen, honey, if you love him, you love him. What's it really matter if he drives an old wreck of a car? What if he is carefree? Isn't that why you liked him from the beginning?"

Irma sank to the bed and grinned. "I guess you're right, Paulette. Maybe I should call him—"

"Sleep on it," Paulette advised. "Let him wait a few hours. It will be good for both of you."

The phone rang. It was Boyd, steaming mad. Poor Boyd! He had sort of been left in the soup.

"I'm leaving in the morning," Boyd said. "I want to see you, Paulette."

"Not tonight," she pleaded.

"For breakfast then. I'll meet you in the dining room at eight."

"All right."

They said goodnight and hung up. Paulette thought of Ross lying in the hospital bed. The whole business was taking on the eeriness of a nightmare. Had it really happened? It had. She knew it had. She had felt Ross' blood on her fingers.

Neither girl thought she would sleep. Irma was certain

she would toss and tumble all night, thinking about Mike, and Paulette didn't think she could forget the horrible scene of Ross lying in the sand, bleeding. But both slept deeply and soundly.

The morning was bright with sunshine. Irma stretched and yawned and reminded Paulette how swiftly their vacation was going. Paulette slipped into a green dress and brushed her red hair until it crackled and shined.

Boyd was in the dining room waiting impatiently. At a nearby table Mike sat, watching for Irma.

"Good morning," Boyd said.

"Hello, Boyd. How are you feeling today?" Paulette asked.

He held the chair for her. "Are you being the nurse again?"

"I've never stopped being one," she reminded him.

"I know," Boyd frowned. "Paulette, are you certain you won't change your mind about me? We'd have a good life together. And I do love you."

"For the moment," she said gently. "Only for the moment. You're not a man who settles down to one thing. Maybe you never will be."

Boyd gripped her hand tightly. "Don't be so sure of that. I would for you."

She took her hand away. "No, Boyd. I'm sorry. I love someone else."

"Ross?"

Her cheeks burned. "Yes."

"The lucky stiff!"

The waiter came to take their order. Her refusal of Boyd didn't seem to affect his appetite. After a few minutes he began to tell her of his next business venture that would take him to Old Mexico.

"I wish you luck, Boyd."

"I'll need it, working for the Old Man," he answered with a grimace.

But she noticed that there was a ring of satisfaction in his voice too.

Breakfast over, he asked her to see him to the limousine

that would take him to the rail station in Sweet Springs. The boy loaded his luggage inside and Boyd handed him a generous tip.

"Well, it seems this is where I came in," he said with a wry smile. There was a hurt, disappointed look in his eyes and she was sorry about that.

"Goodbye, Boyd."

"Goodbye."

He kissed her on the cheek. Then quickly, without a backward look, he climbed into the waiting car. She heard him order the driver to drive away quickly. Her heart tipped a little. Life with Boyd Sheridan would have been interesting. She never doubted that for a moment.

Mike appeared beside her. His grin was as bright as a rainbow. "Come join Irma and me. We have an announcement to make."

Irma's cheeks were flushed pink. Her eyes glowed with happiness. Mike was falling all over himself as he helped Paulette to sit down at their breakfast table.

"Well?" Paulette asked with amused eyes, as if she didn't know what they wanted to tell her.

"She's going to marry me, Paulette. She's really going to marry me!" Mike burst out.

"I'm glad for you," Paulette told them. "I can tell just by looking at you how happy you both are."

"I never figured I'd find a girl like this," Mike confessed. "And I've been looking for some time now."

"Oh, Mike!" Irma giggled. "I'm really not so much. I'm not even pretty."

"Who says you aren't?" Mike asked. "I adore that pug nose, and if there weren't so many looking, I'd kiss you right now."

"I'll arrange a small celebration party," Paulette decided. "I'm sure the hotel can handle it. I'll talk to them about it."

"She's taking me just as I am. A no good saddle bum," Mike kept saying over and over. "Just think of that!"

"So I'm nuts!" Irma shrugged. "I don't care where we live or how we live, as long as we're together, Mike."

Mike grasped Irma's hand tightly in his. "You mean that, don't you?"

"She means it," Paulette spoke up. "Look, I think I should leave you two alone to make plans—"

"No, wait," Mike said with a grin. "I guess it's time I confessed to something. I hope you'll understand, Irma. But I wanted to be sure, that's all. I don't mind telling you, a few women have set their hats for me, because of who I was and for the ranch and everything—but not you. You love me for myself. That's what I want."

"Mike," Irma frowned. "You're not making a bit of sense."

"I'm trying to tell you. I'm not a bum, Irma. And I do have a steady job. I do have better clothes than these, and I do have a Cadillac. I let something slip about that last night, but I guess Paulette was so worried about Ross she never caught it."

"Mike, what are you saying?" Paulette asked.

"I own the third largest ranch in the state. I'm not a poor, extravagant bum. I came here like this, hoping to find a girl that would marry me for myself, not my money. Don't you see?"

Irma's mouth sagged open with shock and Paulette blinked.

"The hotel knows who I am. They've had orders not to tell anyone what they know or I wouldn't ever come back. The Indians, Johnny's parents, knew me as soon as I said my name. They've heard of me. They've heard of my ranch. They also know I employ the Indians, that I do what I can to help them. So—they trusted me—"

"For goodness sakes!" Paulette gasped.

"You mean I'm marrying a—a—"

"Not a millionaire," Mike grinned. "But a man pretty well off. Honey, I want to keep you here, take you to see the ranch and make plans for the wedding. Do you have to go back to Bryson at all?"

Paulette got up and walked away. They hardly knew when she had gone. She was happy for Irma. She had got everything she wanted in a man. But mostly, she had found a true love.

A true love! Paulette's heart jumped, thinking of Ross. But knowing that she loved him didn't mean that it was going to work out as well for her as it had for Irma. That horrible accident would surely drive Ross back to Judith Arnold and New York.

She freshened up in her room and caught the next scheduled limousine to Sweet Springs. Walking to the hospital, she wondered how she would find Ross.

The hospital corridors were quiet. The morning routines hadn't got into full swing yet. A nurse directed her to Ross' room. The door was open. He was propped up in bed, a little pale but awake. His dark eyes searched her face hungrily and he reached out a hand to her.

"Ross, how do you feel?" she asked anxiously.

"Surgery, even minor surgery, isn't my idea of a picnic. But I'm going to be all right. I'm glad you found me when you did. I could have bled to death."

"You shouldn't have gone out there, Ross!"

"I had to. I had to tell them myself how badly I felt about losing Johnny. I was going to tell them about Dave. I was even going to preach at them a little, tell them to consult a doctor immediately the next time sickness cropped up in the family—"

"But it turned out so horribly!"

"He couldn't help it. He acted on impulse. That and whiskey. After Dave died I would have liked to strike out at someone or something just as violently."

His fingers felt cool in her hand. He tugged her closer.

"I'm glad you're here," he said. "Would you mind doing me a favor? My regular nurse is due back to the hotel tomorrow. But until then, would you check on all my patients, tell me how they're doing? Sort of hold the fort for me?"

"If you want. But I'm no doctor."

"But you're a nurse—a very good, human, warm nurse!"

"You'll turn my head with such a compliment!"

"I'll be in the hospital for a week probably," Ross told her.

"I'll be gone by then," she replied.

"Gone?" he asked.

"Yes. Back to Bryson and Bryson General. Back in a white uniform, running up and down those halls—"

She sighed. She dreaded the whole idea of it.

"Don't go," he said quietly. "Don't go, Paulette."

She met his dark eyes. A dozen questions raced through her head.

"I want you to stay," he said. "I want you to team up with me when I move back to Rugged Rock."

"You're staying!" she gasped. "After what happened?"

"Should I turn my back on them because one Indian went a little wild when he lost a son? No. All the more reason to stay, to help prevent that sort of thing from happening again."

"But what about New York, and Judith, and the partnership with her father?"

"I phoned Judith before I went out to see the Indians last night. I told her it was all off. Everything."

"Everything?" Paulette asked.

Ross nodded and pulled her closer. "Everything. I don't love Judith. I don't think I ever did. I belong here, Paulette, and so do you."

"But I'm not sure—"

"I love you," he said. "I love you, Paulette. I need you. I want you to come to Rugged Rock with me."

He reached up and pulled her down until their lips met.

"I love you," he whispered. "Oh, how I love you!"

"And I love you, Ross."

"Will you stay? Will you go with me to Rugged Rock?"

"Yes. I think I knew yesterday, when I went there, that I wanted to stay, to help."

Ross smiled. His fingers traced the outline of her face.

"It won't be easy, darling."

"But I'll have you and you'll have me. What else matters?"

"Nothing," he murmured. "Nothing at all."

If you enjoyed this book, you will want to read these selected romances from the lists of

ACE BOOKS

Three unusual stories of romantic suspense, by one of the outstanding Gothic novelists of our time. . .

THUNDER HEIGHTS by Phyllis A. Whitney (K-158/50¢)

"Thunder Heights is a suspense and love story appealing to those who love Bronte, Du Maurier and Mary Stewart."
—*The Library Journal*

"A romantic tale in the true Gothic tradition." —*Booklist*

THE TREMBLING HILLS by Phyllis A. Whitney (K-164/50¢)

A romantic suspense novel of a young woman in terror of her life in a gloomy San Francisco mansion at the time of the Great Earthquake. "Holds the interest from start to finish."
—*Richmond Times Dispatch*

THE QUICKSILVER POOL by Phyllis A. Whitney (K-178/50¢)

Suspense, romance and danger-filled mystery in a sinister old mansion in which a young bride finds her life and love threatened by a shadowy, nameless danger. "Rebecca-like."
—*Richmond News Leader*

Four more best-selling novels of romantic suspense by ACE STAR:

K-200   **50¢**
THE WHISPER OF SHADOWS by J. L. H. Whitney

Suspense on a windswept island, as a gentle young girl falls in love with her mysterious employer, and is tormented by the fear that he may be responsible for the violent deaths of his wife and secretary, and the brutal attempt on her own life.

K-205   **50¢**
NIGHT OF THE VISITOR by Ruth Willock

A young bride is accidentally separated from her husband, and accepts the grudging hospitality of relatives she barely even knows. While awaiting her husband she discovers that one of her new cousins is a murderer guarding a family secret—and she may well be the next victim.

K-207   **50¢**
A DARK AND SPLENDID PASSION by Lady Eleanor Smith

Lady Eleanor Smith, herself a descendant of one of Britain's oldest families, writes a suspenseful tale of a young bride left alone in the ghost-ridden manor house of her husband's noble family, who finds herself caught in an atmosphere of soul-searing terror and evil as she strives to unlock a fatal secret—the ancient mystery of two star-crossed lovers.

K-209   **50¢**
THE VEIL OF SILENCE by Aileen Seilaz

Installed with her charge in an isolated house in the country, a young governess discovers that she is the final barrier between a murderer and her ward's money—and life.